Mount
Mount, Gail
The man who believed /

34028081052574
KW $15.95 ocn802261777
09/19/12

3 4028 08105 2574
HARRIS COUNTY PUBLIC LIBRARY

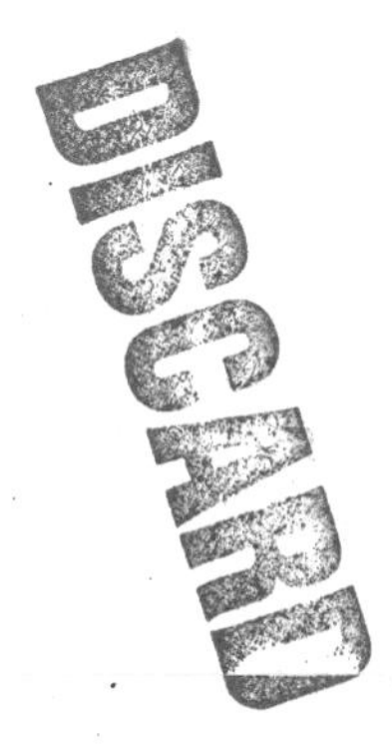

DISCARD

Presented to

Kingwood Branch Library

By

FOLK – Friends of
Library-Kingwood

Harris County
Public Library
your pathway to knowledge

D1387025

Also by Gail Mount

Novel

Pitching Tents

Plays

The Offing

Vicissitudes

The Man Who Believed

The Man Who Believed

Gail Mount

Phosphene Publishing Company
Houston, Texas

The Man Who Believed
© 2011 by Gail Mount
ISBN: 0979696895
ISBN 13: 978-0-9796968-9-3

All rights reserved. No part of this work may be copied or otherwise produced or reproduced in any form, printed or electronic, without express permission, except for brief excerpts used in reviews, articles, and critical works.

Published by
Phosphene Publishing Company
phosphenepublishing.com

To my sons, Frank and Paul Mount

A note of thanks to Professors George Hendrick
and Robert D. Heslep for their comments and suggestions.

Note

This is the story of a man who believed — not always in the same thing but in something. As such it raises the question: do some things such as eating, voiding, evacuating, growing two sets of teeth, having red hair, dying, demand belief or are they so natural belief isn't necessary? If someone asks if you believe in love and you say No or if someone asks what do you believe in and you say Nothing, is nonbelief then an act of believing, a conundrum, a high school word game?

The man, woman or child who believes thinks what he believes is true or has the possibility of being true. He doesn't think what he believes is false or likely false.

The person who believes something is true or likely true will act on it. See Adolf Hitler on the Third Reich, Joseph Stalin on Communism, Adam Smith on the Free Market, Thomas Paine on "The Rights of Man," see the man next door and his neighbor's wife.

Is there then one truth or several? Is it not possible there are several kinds of truth, logical, empirical, theoretical, practical, religious, irreligious, scientific, tragic, comic, fictional? There may be others.

One thing whether or not this novel is true or likely to be true, it is not cynical. It may look like it at times but it's not.

Neither is it false unless, forgive me, the truths of fiction are false.

The Man Who Believed

Origins

Depending on who is telling the story the first time
my mother saw me she said anyone could see I was an idiot and should be put up for adoption.

My Aunt Jenny said Not so. Anyone with a brain could tell by the look on my face I was a comic genius.

My father, a practical man, said it was too early to tell what I was, we'd have to wait and see.

I had moments where it was hard to tell if my actions were those of an idiot or a comic genius.

I didn't learn to walk until the ripe old age of eighteen months, which, my mother said, was further proof I was an idiot.

Aunt Jenny said it proved no such thing, What it proved was I was a comic genius, why walk when I could crawl faster than I could walk. Which after a while turned out not to be the case.

From the time I started walking until I was four I preferred the neighbors' flowerbeds to our bathroom.

My mother said it was more proof I was an idiot, not that more proof was needed. Aunt Jenny said what I left behind was more proof I was a comic genius. My father said when it came to my dung all he knew was if he could sell it we'd get rich. The neighbors' plants had never looked better.

The issue of Flowerbeds versus Indoor Plumbing was resolved when I became toilet trained.

You hear all sorts of stories about how toilet training affects the development of the child. All I know is when I turned four and starting using the bathroom I told my mother goodbye and ran away from home.

I was found in a field of yellow wildflowers feeding a ground rattler to an eagle. The Neighborhood Section of the local newspaper ran an article with picture, Boy Who Ran Away From Home Feeds Ground Rattler to Eagle.

The usual controversy followed, idiot, comic genius or lucky.

The first grade was a watershed year. I learned to add three and two and five and get ten. I had fun playing inspection time with Hilda in the boiler room. We didn't just look. We touched.

I like to think we'd still be playing if Miss Burns hadn't caught us. We were suspended for a week. Hilda's parents fearing what Hilda might become enrolled her in a Roman Catholic school. I heard later she'd become a nun.

My mother told a neighbor she was at her wits end, she didn't know what to do with me. Nothing worked.

Her friend said, You could send the boy to Reform school or you could lock him in a closet. That's what I did. Worked like a charm. My son came out a new boy.

So my mother locked me in a closet.

The theory was the dark coupled with a diet of bread and water would force me to decide if I wanted to live in darkness or the light. In just a few days I'd come out a new me.

My father freed me much to the consternation of my mother after two hours of bread and water and darkness.

Aunt Jenny said she didn't see what all the fuss was about, she'd done the same thing and she wasn't a fallen woman. My mother said there was some doubt about that.

I looked long and hard for a girl to replace Hilda. When I couldn't find one a five year old boy offered to play the girl. The boy looked like a girl but his mother wouldn't have it.

Not much happened in the second, third and fourth grades.

The fifth was different. I was blond, cute, young, studious, frail, the perfect teacher's pet, until Mrs. King caught me and Naomi exchanging love notes. I'd seen my mother when she was upset but I'd never seen her fly into a rage like Mrs. King. The woman threw her favorite glass paperweight against the blackboard. The paperweight didn't break, it bounced off the blackboard and her desk and missed me by a hair before it rattled around on the floor. I was so scared I shit my pants.

At the time I didn't know anything about the theory of unintended consequences. I hadn't intended to soil my britches, I hadn't intended to make the class laugh, I hadn't intended for my romance with Naomi to end, I certainly hadn't intended for her to tell me she couldn't like anyone who went around with soiled britches and I certainly hadn't intended for her to tell me she liked Mitchell better.

The only good thing that happened was as mad as my mother was at me she was madder at Mrs. King.

My father didn't say a thing, he just smiled. Aunt Jenny said I should be proud I'd made the class laugh.

I was thirteen when I got into what could've been serious trouble. The woman across the street and I didn't get along. One night I peeked through her bedroom window (she'd left the window shade up) and saw her naked. I was so intent on watching her I didn't hear the police or my parents.

I was handcuffed and put in the back seat of a patrol car and taken Downtown. The Judge said I'd committed a terrible crime, that a life of crime was a dangerous life, that if I didn't change I would wind up in prison. I might even get killed.

She went on to say I looked like a good, clean cut boy, not some criminal, not some pervert. She said if I were to promise to give up a life of crime, she would find a way to see to it I had a clean record. It was up to me.

Hardly any boy my age had a record. I thought it'd be neat if I had one. The way my father looked at me convinced me I'd be better off without a record. So I promised.

My mother cried, my father said I did the right thing. Aunt Jenny shook her head and said some things are too funny.

Even though I promised No more Peeping Tom, I didn't escape punishment. I mopped floors, waxed the kitchen floor, cleaned the bathroom, washed clothes, raked leaves and mowed the yard. In addition I washed and polished the car.

Despite my father I was locked in the closet at night for a week.

I didn't think about the power of darkness, the power of light, the nature of good and evil, all I thought about was how to give the woman something real to complain about.

Halloween, was the perfect time, her front porch was the perfect place. I found a nice pile of dog crap, put it on a piece of paper and set fire to it on her front porch. I knocked on the door and ran.

I would have gotten away if I'd remembered the big oak stump in her front yard. I hit it shin high, did a flip in mid air and landed face down in the drainage ditch in front of her house.

I'd also forgotten about the ditch filled with recent rain.

I would have drowned if the woman hadn't pulled me out. My mother asked her why she did what she did.

The woman said she didn't know. She'd gotten crap all over her new shoes. The only reason she could think of was I was just a boy.

My life took a turn for the better when I was fourteen. My parents got me a paper route. The idea was I was to develop a sense of responsibility, to learn what had to be done and do it. Last but far from least I was to learn the value of hard earned money, which wasn't all bad.

Not that the job was a piece of cake. A German Shepherd chased me every day until I squirted him with ammonia. Worse were my customers who on collection day did their best to make me feel like I was taking food from the mouths of their children.

The best thing about the job other than when I quit was the sleepy-eyed, long haired blonde who always came to the door with collection money in hand and nothing on but her see through bra and panties. She never failed to ask how I was. She never failed to say she'd invite me in but she had to take a shower. When I suggested I join her, she allowed that was a good idea, but that it would take too long, she didn't want to be late for work. Next time, for sure.

Next time for sure never came. I learned when a woman says 'Next time for sure,' in her mind it's the same thing as having done it. One morning I asked if it had been as good for her as it was for me. She smiled.

Sex was everywhere but out of reach.

Fifteen wasn't all bad. The girl in the house on the corner was born with a baby fat charm. When she turned fourteen, her baby fat charm turned into breasts, legs with calves and a rear end to die for.

She loved to ride her bicycle in her gym suit. One day when my father and I were driving home from the store she smiled and turned so we could see what big breasts she had.

My father said, "Is that Evelyn?"

I said "Yes."

He said, "The way she sits on the seat.... She put out?"

I said, "Yes."

He said, "You ever?"

I said, "No."

He said, "Better not to rush some things."

I didn't have to worry about that.

Sex was everywhere but still out of reach.

What made it painful was I kept coming close. This girl and I were necking in the Balcony of the Majestic and she moaned. Taking that as a sign I ran my hand up her skirt and pulled her pants down. She screamed. Later she told me she thought my hand was a mouse.

The upshot was I was still a virgin when I graduated.

College

was different.

My freshman year, thanks to a girl named Jane, I and a hundred other boys lost their virginity without having to beg. She also gave me my first blowjob.

I felt good in ways I never imagined. So good I wanted to tell my parents and our preacher they were wrong about sex, sex wasn't a sin, sex was great.

My sophomore year I discovered Jonathan Swift and his statement, "What Humor is, not all the Tribe of Logick-mongers can describe." I found my dream. I wrote jokes and satires for *Suppressed Desires*, the campus humor magazine. Things like:

Marriage and trade came first. Adultery and false accounting practices followed.

How long is a piece of string?

Did Jesus ever do anything His Mother didn't want him to?

If mankind, women and men, children and adolescents, truly love religious wars, if God and organized killing are essential, if purity and punishment are necessary, if looking for immortality and the death of friends and enemies keep us going, no wonder life is a tragedy up close and a comedy at a distance.

Is it fucking hopeless or is it hopeless fucking?

Like a minor Swift, a minor Flaubert, a minor Conrad I sat for twenty-four hours, struggling, looking for a word other than fucking, only to decide fucking was the word.

I was put on probation for a year, *Surpressed Desires* for three.

My junior year I was young and passionate and so was Marian. We were so passionate that on our first date we got naked and quarreled about the purpose of sex, without having sex. Marian said Procreation. I said Pleasure.

No telling what would have happened if I'd said Procreation but I never did. I was too high minded.

I said, "What about sex for the sake of sex, Sex for no reason at all, sex that has nothing to do with procreation, sex that provides sundry pleasures, masturbation, fellatio, cunnilingus, homosexual sex, anal, spanking, being spanked, flogging, being fluffed, tied up, handcuffed to the bed, bestiality, doing it to be doing it, out of a sense of obligation, love, a desire to comfort, for meanness, for no reason at all."

She called me a degenerate. I told her I wasn't a degenerate, I was a young man trying to get laid and not doing too well. She said she could see why.

My senior year was a different sort of fun. I ran into Marian on the Quad. She was all smiles. "I've been meaning to call you. You were right. I've found pleasure without any thought of procreation and it is good. Thank you. Bye-bye."

As if that wasn't enough my Professor-Tutor insisted that the rest of my life depended on what I did on my Senior Thesis, a hundred page analysis of What Does It Profit A Man To Gain The Whole World?

I started to say "A lot" but settled for, "I have no idea."

Because of that and my attitude (I laughed when the President of the University handed me my diploma) I didn't graduate.

My parents couldn't have been more understanding. They gave me a suitcase and a check for a thousand dollars and told me I could no longer live at home, but to write when I found work and got settled.

I had trouble finding a job. I don't know what I'd have done if I hadn't come across one of our class rings in a pawn shop. I might have become the bum my father predicted.

The ring was more than a ring, people would see the ring and think I had a first class degree from a first class university. Even with the ring I needed written proof.

I could have done the honorable thing and repeated my senior year.

The result, a diploma, an app to graduate school, a revised

transcript, two letters of recommendations, and a resume. The app required an essay. I called it "The New Dark Ages." I have a copy somewhere.

Later, my friend embezzled millions from the Endowment, paid a portion back and agreed to go forth and sin no more. The last I heard he bought an island in the Caribbean where he lives in peace and contentment.

Wonder of wonders I was admitted to

Graduate School

In retrospect my lie didn't do much harm. My lying actually had a positive outcome.

For the first time in the history of the English Department there weren't enough students with M.A.'s to qualify as teaching assistants. The department after much soul searching decided if you were a graduate student in English who had a B.A. but no M.A. you could apply for a T/A and if selected (Little chance you wouldn't be) you could help teach the mass of new freshmen who were flooding the University.

Freshman English and the world would be better off.

The only problem was what would happen if the Department found out how I got my B.A. A literal minded professor who believed rules should be rules and enforced no matter the consequences fought to keep me from being hired.

Fortunately he was committed for wandering around in his underwear babbling about the Godhead.

The Department said I'd been seen talking to the man on more than one occasion. What did we talk about?

I figured what the Department didn't know wouldn't hurt them. I said the weather. Thus I became a T/A.

My first year I was the silliest T/A imaginable. I followed a budget. I signed up for three seminars leading to a PhD. I studied two hours for every hour spent in class. I made all A's. I devoted forty hours a week to grading papers and preparing lectures.

My second year I wasn't so silly. I discovered The Dive, one of the world's great beer joints, home to jocks who liked to drink beer and fight and fuck; and to girls who liked to drink beer and fuck jocks; and students like me who liked to drink beer, watch jocks fight, and dream of screwing the girls the jocks screwed.

I couldn't fight, I didn't screw one girl who'd slept with one jock. But I discovered I could make money on the side by tutoring, by writing papers and by being able to drink ten beers, twelve to fifteen if money was at stake. I never lost.

And while I never slept with a girl who had slept with a jock, I was never completely celibate.

—⊹—

A hard to resist freshman who looked like she'd stepped out of a Rubens showed up at my hole in the wall apartment in the middle of the night, asking if I had a bathroom, she had to pee in the worst way.

I said I had a bathroom.

She said she needed a place to sleep.

I said I had a bed.

She said I'll do anything you want, I mean anything, anything, you name it.

A female T/A had been kicked out that very week for sleeping with one of her students.

Rubens slept in the bed. I slept in the bathtub.

She called to thank me for putting her up. She told me she'd decided to leave the university, it wasn't for her.

The last time I saw her we made love in the backseat of her car in a rainstorm.

—⊹—

My best friend's fiancee called. "Want to go skinny dipping?"

"I might. When?"

"Tonight."

"Who all's going?"

"If you go, the two of us."

"The two of us. Where?"

"Hidden Spring."

"What about Jim?"

"What about Jim? I need to do something different. I want to be with somebody different, I need to talk to somebody different, that's you. It'll be our secret. What Jim doesn't know won't hurt Jim. Look, if you don't want to go, say so."

I said, "I didn't say I didn't want to go."

She said, "Good. If we're lucky we'll have it all to ourselves. If not, we'll make do."

We were lucky.

She shucked her clothes and stood in front of me naked. I didn't think how lucky my best friend Jim was I thought how lucky I was.

I wasn't much to look at with my clothes on. My skinny legs, my sunken chest and a burgeoning paunch weren't much to look at. I started to apologize for my body. She stopped me with a kiss. We made love without saying a word.

She wrapped her legs around me and said "Daddy had a heart attack but God spared him."

I said, "I'm glad She did."

She laughed, "Be serious."

I said, "A comic genius is always serious."

She laughed.

We took turns making love and napping until dawn. The sunrise woke us up.

She said, "I wish I could stay here all day. But I can't." She grinned, "Tell you what, let's make love in the water one more time."

The water was cold enough to make our teeth chatter. We took turns drying each other off. She enjoyed rubbing my skin raw. Drying her off was almost as good as making love.

She and Jim were married the last day of the month. I was Jim's Best Man.

For the poignantly romantic I never saw them again.

Carole also known as Willowy Campus Sweetheart had platinum blonde hair, dark eyes, long legs, small breasts, a tightly wound rear and a face that lit up like sudden light.

She didn't just walk in beauty, she was Joi de vivre.

The first time we met she was looking for a tutor. I told her I used to charge five dollars an hour to tutor and twenty-five to write a paper, but I was no longer in the business.

She said she didn't need me to write anything for her, she wanted to know what I thought about the current crop of literary critics.

I said the thing about most critics today is they are so committed to a set of rules and principles they got from someone else they don't know a goddamned thing.

She snorted, "Who told you that?"

I said I did.

We dated for a semester. The only time we made love was graduation night. That same night she told me she could never marry me because I'd never be a financial success. She was going to marry a man everyone said would be governor.

A month after their European honeymoon Willowy Campus Sweetheart called to say she'd discovered the man everyone thought would be Governor had rather drink than be Governor or make love but she'd found a matador in Spain who liked to drink and make love, and who unlike me was good at it.

Not long after she made headlines when she left the former Governor to be and the matador, for a female evangelist.

The two wrote a book, *The Lasting Love of Jesus*. The parts on how to love aren't bad.

I decided I might as well get my Master's even though I was there under false pretenses.

I wrote a short novel, *Where the Light Is as Darkness*, in two weeks. I turned it in to my advisor the day after it was due. The man gave me a C, graduate school polite for an F. He refused to listen to my pleas for a B minus, which meant no Master's.

The Chairperson of The Committee on T/A's called and said she'd like to see me at her office at eight thirty in the morning.

That night at The Dive over a beer I told a friend who would soon have his PhD. "Tomorrow is coup de grace day, the day I find out if I'm to be a T/A next year."

My friend whose dissertation was on the wit and wisdom of Polonius, decided to share his wit and wisdom with me:

"Be a penitent, but not a sycophant, be a supplicant but not a beggar, be humble but not obsequious, be cunning but not a snake, be proud but not arrogant.

"Suggest delicious delights being careful not to be rash. Show her your tongue, not your loins until the right moment and failing that and all else be evasive like The Great Man and tell her to go screw herself then get your ass the hell out of there and into the real world."

I said you always tell others to get out of the academic world while you hold on for dear life.

He smiled and said, "Fortunes of war."

The woman looked at me over her glasses, "I'm Dr. Koch. Please sit."

Her phone rang. She said, "Pardon me I need to answer this. If this is who I think it I'm going to be a while. Make yourself at home."

I tried not to listen, but I couldn't help but overhear, "He's here. I'll call you after I've read his file and we have finished our business."

I didn't feel so good.

I looked around. Walt Whitman smiled at me from on high. Mark Twain gave me his best ironic grin. Theodore Dreiser didn't look any too happy. Neither did Thoreau. Hart Crane looked like he was trying to decide if he should go for a swim. Thomas Wolfe was either getting on or getting off a train. John Steinbeck looked embarrassed at having his picture taken. William Faulkner looked like an English Dandy. Hemingway looked like he'd just farted. The only woman, Edna St. Vincent Millay, smiled confident she could outlast any ten men.

Dr. Koch and the guy on the other end of the line were still going at it.

She put a handkerchief over the mouthpiece and whispered, "Help yourself to a book."

With that I got up and went over to her full to the brim bookcase.

I had never read her *The Rebel Hero in American Literature*, but there it was staring at me. The story was Dr. Koch should have won the Pulitzer Prize, but some other guy won it.

I'd read her next, *Be Grateful for the Rebellious*. I expected a call to arms, what I got was it was okay for teenagers to be rebellious, but not sensible adults, a popular idea at the time.

I took *The Rebel Hero* and went back and sat down. I skimmed chapters on active rebels, passive rebels, contrite rebels, reformed rebels, nonrebels. I wasn't sure what kind of rebel I was, active, passive, contrite, reformed or non. I assumed I was in there somewhere.

She hung up and gave me the once over.

I hadn't worn a suit or sportscoat. Instead, I'd worn what I considered my one vanity, my one and only Brooks Brothers shirt. Despite being accused of having a button down mind I liked the button down collar and the feel of Oxford cloth.

I always wore the shirt sans tie, open at the neck, with my sleeves rolled up to show my biceps. I was tough.

That day was no different.

Dr. Koch said, "Like your shirt. Where's your tie?"

I said, "At home. I'd heard your field was Whitman, so I thought you preferred casual."

She said, "Well said. Sorry about the delay, since you went to the trouble to be on time. Being punctual is a virtue and today you were virtuous."

It was her way of telling me I was in for it.

She smiled, "I want you to know whatever else you may have done these past two years, you have left your mark on the University. Thanks to you, today's T/A's dress worse than any bum. You should be proud." I thanked her.

She said, "Ever been to a psychiatrist?"

I said, "No."

She said, "Anyone ever tell you, you have a death wish?"

"No."

"Then why begin your eight o'clock by having everyone stand and repeat ten times, 'I'm a mammal.'"

"It's an eight clock. They're freshmen, they need something to get them going. Besides there are two girls who need to remind themselves they're mammals."

She said, "That's something. You're something."

I said, "So are you. You have an uncanny resemblance to Frieda Lawrence. You two could be twins. I've always admired her. She's a great woman." I couldn't help myself I added 'too."

The Dr. Koch the Professor took over. She said with more than a touch of iron in her voice, "I'm frequently mistaken for her twin but as you can see I'm not her twin. As for being great that's not for me to say.

"So I may get a better feel for what's going on, what did you tell the Dean of Humanities when he asked you what you talked about in class?"

"I told him 'Nothing, everything, anything to stimulate the class, sex, religion. Communism, football, alcohol, the assignment.'"

She said, "Anything to stimulate the class. Admirable. What'd the Dean say?"

"He said Bullshit in academic lingo."

She said, "Did he? Bless his heart. I understand my friend the Dean. But I don't understand you. Your first year, you were exemplary. Every one of your students passed the Final. You made all A's in your classes. You saw your advisor at least once a quarter. The second year you did a hundred eighty. You cut Chaucer three weeks in a row. Why?"

"The man made Chaucer boring."

"How many times did you see your advisor?"

"Once, this year."

"Once? This year?"

"That was enough."

Dr. Koch said, "I'll never understand why you wanted a Master's in Creative Writing."

"I was a better writer than anyone else around."

"You'd have been a lot better off if you'd done your work under me."

To me the idea of working under Dr. Koch made no sense. I shouldn't have laughed but I did. I should have apologized. But I didn't.

She said, "No matter, it's too late. Anyway to cut to the chase I have bad news and worse news. Some of your students have complained to their Daddies, their Daddies have complained to the Department. Some of their Daddies are ready to go to their Legislators."

Dr. Koch gave me her best serious smile. "You've made a lot of enemies in the Department, some with your mouth, some because you haven't made sufficient progress toward the PhD. Any comment?"

"I'll have a talk with my mouth but I did pass the Qualifying Exam."

Dr. Koch said, "Wasn't that the silliest exam you ever saw?"

I said, "I thought it was a good exam."

"Did you?"

"Yes."

She said, "You may be right. Let me tell you what gets my goat. During Religious Emphasis Week while other Freshman English classes were writing papers on 'The Importance of Religion in Education' yours were writing papers on 'The Virtues of Leading a Pagan Life.'"

"Sorry. Seemed like a good idea at the time."

"It's too late for sorry and as for its being a good idea at the time or any time, The English Department, The School of Humanities and The Administration feel this is a good idea, it's time for you to move on."

I said, "What do you think?"

"You've left me no choice but to agree."

I said, "Anything to make Daddy happy. Oh, well, might as well get it over with. Any idea when?"

She said, "What about today?"

I said, "Good as any."

She said, "As good as any. Wonderful. Sayonara, Adios, auf Wiedersehen, Au revoir, toodle-loo, goodbye, good luck. Don't come back. No hard feelings."

I said, "No hard feelings, I love this place."

That day was not only my last day at the University, that night was my last at The Dive. I was five beers suave when this blonde out of a Mickey Spillane novel sidled up to me.

I said, "Buy you a beer."

She said, "I'm twenty-six and divorced. I've had bad days, but today takes the cake. I failed my orals this afternoon, for the second time, the second time, after my advisor promised me there was no way I could fail. The kind of relief I need is more than alcohol can give. I hope to God you're up to it."

She was cold sober smooth. She liked to make love to the rhythm of a metronome. I had trouble keeping time.

If I hadn't made her laugh the night would have been a disaster.

So, there I was dumped out of the lap that was Graduate School onto what people called the world. What was I to do?

I couldn't move back home.

Friends wouldn't take me in.

I had no desire to sleep under another viaduct.

I didn't have much choice, R.A., or life on the lam.

I went R.A. The army decided I was more of a threat in than out. Someone came up with the idea of an Honorable Discharge, although a Colonel insisted I be Discharged For The Good of the Service. Fortunately for me, he lost.

With my Honorable Discharge in hand I went to Mexico. A beautiful country with strong men, sexy women, great art, too many hard lives and too much bad pulque. I loved Mexico, but it was no place for me.

Frost chose his road, I chose mine.

Show Business

Hollywood!

I had a plan. Turn *Where the Light Is as Darkness* into a screenplay. Sell it to a studio. Write others. Sell them. Plenty of money, get laid any time I felt the need. No hill for a climber. Simple.

Not so simple. My only offer came from a producer of porn. She wasn't looking to buy a screenplay, she was looking for new talent, and I was the man. The idea was the female star would make love to me with a strap on. The scene would make porno history.

My life was dark, was it ever. I needed the money bad. I surprised myself when I said "No, thanks."

The problem was what to do next. Then as if God cared, my agent called with a question, "Are you good, not any good, in bed?"

I said "The worst."

She said, "Report to Sheba Reba at the BellyLaff. She won't know the difference."

Sheba Reba took one look at me, "You're blond, you have a nice face, great eyes, a sexy mouth, and a great smile. I hope to God you're funny."

I said, "I'm as funny as The BellyLaff hunting for a fire."

She said, "Now, that's funny."

The former combination house of worship-gambling-dance-hall-saloon was the place you went when you wanted to meet your maker. As times changed the BellyLaff became a hotel with rooms for rent by the day, week, month or hour with or without bath, with or without man or woman. It was Hollywood.

After a cop shut the BellyLaff down because he didn't think his take was enough the BellyLaff became a French Restaurant, a picture show showing B movies, then in an unmatched display of social responsibility, a town hall, a porno film palace and now as its Marquee said "The Home of Beginners' Luck Nite, A Nite of Surreal & Different Comedy."

Sheba Reba, lover of rhyme, six foot Mistress of Ceremony, enforcer, survivor, with the shapeliest big breasts you could imagine pulled one out of her gown and said "I wonder what the butts in the seats will think when they see this beauty."

The butts in the seats, rednecks, roughnecks, husbands on a night out looking for whatever, wives on a night out looking for whatever, shipping clerks, doctors, lawyers, executives with their office nieces, teachers, college students on a lark, men in funny suits, professors and deep thinkers, whistled and yelled and stamped their feet.

Sheba Reba smiled, "My kind of people. Wish me luck."

Sheba Reba's right breast kept popping out like it had a life of its own.

She gave the audience a sideways look, "Jesus Lord, I'd hate to step on my own tit. Come to think of it that would be something to see."

A trumpet shrieked, a drum rolled. Sheba Reba shook, she undulated. She grabbed a bottle of Evian and made swallowing from the bottle look like fellatio.

The audience stomped and whistled.

She reholstered her breast. "Welcome to Beginner's Luck Nite, an evening of Surreal and Different Comedy at The BellyLaff."

The audience whistled and clapped and stomped. Echoes followed and the floor shook.

Sheba Reba said, "If my beauties keep falling out we could be here all night. Great thing breasts, but this beauty here," she blew her V a kiss, "is what tries men's souls."

The audience came apart.

Sheba Reba said, "Enough about me. Time for our first performer. A believe it or not single parent, a multicultural mother of four by four, white, brown, yellow, black, with a big heart, a soul to match and a body that makes brick shithouses jealous.

"Put your hands together, give it up, show your love for Ms. Susie Dildeaux, that's D-i-l-d-e-a-u-x, for those who can't spell."

I expected a roly-poly woman, but Susie was a young well put together five foot, ninety pounds. Susie slithered across the floor like a cobra, bounced up and vibrated in a way that made me squirm.

A red dildo appeared from out of nowhere and slid up and down her body, between her breasts, her buttocks and her legs. She popped her pelvis and the dildo flew across the stage like a missile.

The audience let go.

Susie bowed and bounced off, dildo in hand.

Rafters shook.

Susie winked at Sheba Reba and said, "Think I'll make it in Hollywood?"

Sheba Reba shook her head, "With an act like yours I don't see how you can miss" then to me, "Jeez, can't anybody wait?"

Sheba Reba said, "Our next act, Loon, is more than a red-headed-pimply-faced-high school nerd dressed as a White Crested Loon. Loon is new comedy."

While the audience was trying to figure out what Sheba Reba meant, Loon strutted across the stage, grabbed the mike, cried the beautiful cry of the loon and said,

"A poem by Loon:

"Waste

"Alpha and Omega

"Beginning and end

"Breakfast food."

Loon let out another mournful cry.

The audience quieted like they were in the presence of genius. I felt like I was in church.

Loon didn't move. He couldn't. He was frozen.

The audience began to giggle.

Susie went to get him.

Loon relaxed his grip on the mike and held onto Susie. He smiled, "I have my driver's license and I'm not a virgin."

Half of the audience sat on their hands, the other half gave the frozen-faced Loon a standing ovation.

Sheba Reba didn't miss a beat.

"Get ready for our next act, a big man up from the primeval pond, Big Bubber!"

Big Bubber oozed on stage like molasses.

He licked his blacker than black lips, "I'se Big Bubber, the new gene pool. Want to go for a swim? No. Want to hear something funny?"

A guy in the audience said, "That's what we came for."

Big Bubber said, "I'll tell you. I'm alive when I should be dead. Lak you. Imagine, six hundred pounds of black me falling on you. A helluva way to get religion. My Daddy never had no religion until I fell on him." He laughed, "It was almost too late."

The audience didn't know what to think. Neither did I.

Big Bubber said, "The trouble with White Folks is they think Black Folks should be a copy of White Folks. Like Sporting Life said, 'What you read in the Bible, ain't necessarily so.'"

Serenity flooded Big Bubber. He turned a slow shuffle into a soft shoe, the soft shoe into a buck-and-wing, the buck-and-wing into joy.

He grinned and rolled his eyes.

Big Bubber never saw what hit him. He flailed and bit his tongue. He twitched. His knees buckled. He grabbed himself and fell in a heap. He didn't move.

The audience sat still.

Sheba Reba ran to him, "Big Bubber, you poor man, you all right?"

Big Bubber said, "Didn't mean to get serious on you."

Sheba Reba kissed him and said, "'Sall right, Big Bubber. Serious is best."

Big Bubber smiled and died.

It took me and five other men to load Big Bubber onto the gurney.

The audience gave Big Bubber a standing O as he was wheeled away.

Sheba Reba hadn't moved. I managed to help her off. The audience applauded.

Susie said, "Big Bubber had a heart bigger than me."

Sheba Reba said, "Big Bubber had an instrument bigger than your dildo."

I said "I wonder how that'll look on his tombstone."

Sheba Reba said, "You're terrible."

Loon said, "Miss Sheba Reba I told the driver to take Big Bubber to the hospital morgue."

Sheba said, "Thank you, Loon. Someone has to tell the audience the man's dead. You there."

"Me?"

"Yes, you, Mr. Six Foot, Blonde and Pretty. You tell them Big Bubber's dead, that the show will go on as a tribute. But no refunds. I mean it. Be quick and be funny."

Be quick and be funny, words fit for a family motto, words to cherish, to remember, to take with me to the grave, easy enough to say, hard to do.

I couldn't have felt more naked.

The next act, a seventy-plus-look-alike Marlene Dietrich in a trench coat, gave me a hug and rubbed my back and said, "Let me."

She took her trench coat off, folded it and put it down. She stood there smiling in her red slip with nothing on underneath.

The audience snickered like children.

She curtseyed and said, "I'm Iris-Isis, philosophical ecdysiast supreme, ontological stripping is my game. I'm here to tell you Big Bubber's dead and will be for a while. But before he passed he said he wanted the show to go on."

The audience giggled.

"It's true. I wouldn't lie to you."

The audience clapped.

She smiled and said, "Here's an example of the meaning of existence: The show is going go as a tribute to Big Bubber and you ain't gonna get your money back. So relax and enjoy."

A guy in the audience yelled, "Lady, where in Hell did you come from?"

Iris-Isis reached in the Trench Coat and pulled out a pistol, She fired two shots into the ceiling, "Now that I have your attention, On with the Show."

Iris-Isis moved across the stage to the universal rhythms of drums. "My father wanted twins. I'm the twins. Iris, messenger to the gods, Isis, wife and sister of Osiris. You know the god who kept getting killed and coming back to life. A cycle of murder, death and resurrection. Sound familiar? Wanta see a seventy-plus year old do a bump and grind?"

The way Iris-Isis moved I thought she was going to dislocate a hip.

The audience lost it. She did another. A guy cried, "Take it off."

Iris-Isis laughed. "Before I do, I want to tell you a true story of chaos and chance. Really.

"My car broke down on the freeway. You have no idea what it is to lose power in the middle of the freeway with one eighteen wheeler roaring down the freeway like water through a hole.

"Somehow, thanks to chance, chaos, a Guiding Hand, a break in the traffic I had no sooner made it across the freeway when this guy stops and opens a door and says, 'I've never screwed a ghost. Here's a hundred. Get in.'"

The audience might not have dug the ontological, they might not have dug Osiris, they may not have dug Chaos and Chance, but they dug sex on the freeway.

Iris-Isis said, "I was about to get in this angel's car when this motorcycle cop stopped and offered me a ride. He couldn't have been twenty-one. I've always been a sucker for a young cop on a motorcycle.

"We left the man who wanted to have sex with a ghost wondering what happened. I kept the hundred."

Not only had I never heard such a story, I'd never heard an audience roar.

Iris-Isis smiled, "We went down a road as dark as a river at night until we found a place where we could make love and watch white caps on the Pacific.

"The young cop was wise beyond his years. He had a quilt and a bottle of Wild Turkey. The quilt was comfortable, the Wild Turkey was good and so was the sex. I prayed it wouldn't be the last time I'd wrap my legs around a young cop with a machine, a quilt and a bottle of Wild Turkey."

The audience had a fit.

Iris-Isis took a deep breath, "A moment ago I gave you an example of the meaning of existence.

"Here's one more profound. A woman's vulva."

Iris-Isis wiggled out of her slip and stood there shock naked.

The audience was petrified.

The young cop carried her off.

I didn't say a word.

The house went dark.

Everybody went home.

The scene was like a scene in a movie only real.

Sheba Reba turned the house lights back on. "I'd like to hear your act. But first tell me your secret ambition."

I said, "For real?"

Sheba Reba said, "What is this, high school?"

I said, "Okay. My secret ambition is I want to connect the longings and feelings in me with the longings and feelings of others through comedy. I believe everything is related, part of a whole. I also tell jokes."

Sheba Reba said, "Such as?"

"L.A. invented fucking but New York will fuck you in a minute.

"Why is a kiss like calcium? It'll raise a bone.

"Woman with two vibrators: Oh oh oh oh oh oh oh oh oh oh

"ooh, ooh, ooh, ooh, ooh, ooh, ooh, ooh, ooh, ooh.

"Ahhhhhhhhhhhhhhhhhhhhhhhhhhhhhhhhhhhh ah.

"Memememe memememe memememe Me!

"Man with penile pump: Goddamn goddamngoddamn Goddamn!

"God was really upset. She said, 'What do you think you're doing? You made me wet my panties. There'll be no more of that. The world is going to Hell in a hand basket as it is."

Sheba Reba laughed. "Shows talent but needs work."

She stretched. Her breasts were like an upheaval of mountains.

She looked at me, "Here it is two o'clock in the morning. What do you say we make love? I'm in the mood."

I said, "Sounds nice but I don't have the energy."

She said, "You gay?"

I said, "Not at the moment."

Sheba Reba said, "Not my night, is it?

The night may not have been Sheba Reba's, but to me it was like a dream.

The BellyLaff burned down the next week. A week later Aunt Jenny died doing stand up at the home.

I should have been there. She was my inspiration and she loved me.

I didn't know what I was going to do. I was about to cash in what few chips I had when my agent, bless her heart, found a small producer of CD's, Make It New, run by a woman who claimed to be the female Ezra Pound of the business.

She said, "Tell me if you're not up to this. I want somebody, maybe you, to march down the middle of Hollywood Boulevard wrapped in Old Glory saying anything that comes to mind. That's anything. I will pay any fines or penalties, post any bond, provided what you say isn't seditious. Not only that I will pay for any burial or hospital expenses in case you get run over or are beaten by the cops or any other law enforcement agent or agency with absolute power to administer beatings."

She smiled, "Seeing someone being beaten by anyone with absolute power is funny. If it's you it's not. Another thing, the pay's good."

I thanked her for the chance. I made a dry run, then one for real. Not one word. Nada. Nothing.

The producer said "Get someone else."

That's all it took. I needed the money.

I took off all my clothes and paraded around naked spewing words as they came.

Pussy Pussy

Screw responsibility before it screws you.

God, it feels good when it stings.

Yea, yea, yay, tea, tay, tay, izzle, sizzle, fizzle,

Swizzle.

You would think science would come up with a stronger word for the male whip than penis.

A man doesn't knock his penis with the world, he knocks his dick with the world. A man doesn't knock another man's penis in the dirt, he knocks the man's dick in the dirt.

It isn't penis head or penis nose, it's dick head, prick nose.

Anything other than John Thomas is better than penis, even wee-wee.

Comediennes have rendered the penis flaccid, but not whip or mule or one-eyed snake, weapon, Anaconda, rod, roll of tar paper, dick. Lennie and Johnson aren't in the running. Ask any thirteen-year-old boy.

I said, "Then there are the various names for the female complex, pussy, vulva, snatch, twat.

I was about to say what a terrible word cunt was when the cop said I was under arrest for profaning sacred words.

I'd always thought it'd be romantic to be handcuffed. It wasn't.

I'd always thought those orange jailhouse uniforms were romantic. They weren't.

Neither was the sound of my cell door slamming shut.

Fortunately my attorney who knew little law was friends with the judge.

"Your Honor, my client didn't shout fire in the middle of a theatre. He was practicing a comic routine."

The Judge said, "The next time your client feels the urge to practice his routines in public tell him to pick some place other than the middle of the street. Case dismissed."

The producer was ecstatic. She wanted a street piece on Shit.

I needed the money. Man, did I.

I grabbed a flag and got after it:

"Used to be men couldn't talk without saying Shit, but now, women have joined the men which should make everybody happy, seeing as how it's one instance in which women and men are equal.

"The act at its best is an old and welcomed friend, as satisfying as eating or making love. At its worst, it's like a sprinkler gone amok, worse still, painful, like giving birth to something dead.

"Think what our language would be without 'shit.' No batshit, no bullshit, no cowshit, catshit, goatshit, horseshit, no baby shit'

"Shit is omnipresent. It's on everyone's tongue, toddlers learning to talk say it, mothers, fathers, grandparents, godparents, teachers, Presidents, ministers, elders, deacons, prostitutes, pimps, lawyers, bankers, priests, nuns, Popes, professors, protectors of the language say it. Those who have taken vows of silence think it.

"What we do without, 'I wouldn't Shit you' or 'Don't Shit a Shitter.'

"There you have it, the last word on 'Shit.'"

I was having such a good time I didn't hear the ambulance and I didn't feel the needle.

I was completely out of it, until I woke up in the Psychiatric Ward of a hospital. When I tried to explain I wasn't crazy and didn't belong there the head nurse said, "Be grateful you're not in with the criminally insane."

A month of sameness passed, one month of cold gray walls, one painting of a burned out cornfield, a view of the gray wall of the building next door, no visitors, a month of ekgs, eegs, MRIs, CAT scans, and questions:

The man asked, "Do you hear voices?"

I said, "I hear yours."

"I mean other voices, unusual voices, voices from beyond with strange messages."

I said, "There was my roommate."

"Oh?"

"I never knew his name but he was a handsome black guy about fifty. He spent 24/7 rocking back and forth and chanting, 'In God we trust.'"

The doctor looked at the nurse.

She said, "He was moved to a long term care facility."

The doctor asked? Still chanting?"

The nurse said, "Still chanting."

The doctor said, "Too bad" then turned to me. "Do you remember breaking down, whathappened, what you were doing? Do you know where you live," Who's President, which century is this? What do you think about electricity?" He didn't mean rural electrification.

I didn't answer.

"Nurse, I want you to see to it our friend here takes his medications. I'll check back in a week. By then we should know if the meds have done the job or if he will need ECT."

I thought some choice, become a medicated zombie or go around with a I'm-all-right smile and no short term memory.

In no time I learned to go around with a I'm-all-right-smile without taking my meds. I'd hide them under my tongue, then when no one was looking, I'd spit them out and flush them.

One nice thing, I didn't have a roommate, but I wasn't lonely. It got to where it was nothing to wake up in the middle of the night and find a naked, pinched face, skinny blonde in bed with me.

"They say I screw too much. I'll show them. I'll begin with you."

The Police Chief of San Diego said he'd have to arrest me if I didn't leave the woman alone.

The President of the United States said he'd pardon me.

The woman soon tired of me. She and the Pope began sneaking into the playroom at night. The Pope would loll around on the pool table while she confessed her sins and did penance.

A boy about sixteen asked if I knew anything about geography. I said a little. He said, "Please tell me where I am. I need to know where the fuck I am."

I sent him to the Nurses' Station.

An elderly woman thought I was her father.

The week passed and the doctor said, "We think your condition may be inherited. Is there any way we can get in touch with your parents?"

I said, "It wouldn't do any good. I don't have a job. Besides they're crazy."

The head nurse said, "With an attitude like that you are in danger of eternal damnation."

The Doctor said, "Do you believe in God?"

I surprised myself the way I said, "No."

"Do you believe in an Uncreated Creator?"

I said, "That's a different question."

The doctor felt my head and looked in my eyes, "The only trace I can find of mental illness is you think you're sane. That's good enough for me, God help us. Adios. You're out of here."

It wasn't long before I half wished I was back in.

Limbo

I quit trying to connect longings and feelings. I worked as a waiter. I was the oldest mail boy in creation, the oldest temporary secretary. I was the one guy in a highway gang that worked. I was the anglo who cut grass and raked leaves. People became suspicious.

I scoured highways for cans.

I begged. A local TV station caught my act.

My agent got me a prime spot on the TV show Open Mike. I'd turned the corner.

The show was cancelled.

There were no other offers. I was living proof a person is not always responsible for what happens to him.

After nothing but tomato soup and ice water for a month the time had come to move to something different.

Even so I didn't plan to give up comedy completely.

After all I was young, maybe not all that young but young.

Maturity?

Talk about belief, I got married without a full time job.

My parents said they were happy for us but we couldn't live with them and they weren't going to support us.

I would have been all right if my friends hadn't stopped lending me money and if my wife hadn't quit work and if her parents who were killed on their way to Tahoe when their car ran off the road and tumbled down a mountain in a snowstorm had had more life insurance.

What money there was didn't last long. I had no choice but to go to work for a firm on Wall Street evaluating contracts.

Thanks to rent control and a key bribe my wife and I lived in an apartment in Brooklyn Heights. On good days I could walk to work in forty-five minutes via the Brooklyn Bridge. The view from the bridge and the walk helped keep me sane.

One morning wondering if I needed therapy, I stopped to watch the naked Japanese girl with hair down to the middle of her back and breasts that looked like cones fix her breakfast.

I lingered and lingered and lingered. Then I heard the first warning rumble. I told myself I'd be okay, that if I couldn't control my bowels what could I control.

By the time I got to the middle of the bridge it was crisis time. I turned around and headed for the bar at the foot of the bridge. Fortunately it was open twenty-four hours a day, I could use their facilities. Unfortunately the bar was closed due the death of the owner.

I remembered a place in the park the homeless used.

That morning two boys were using it to fight. Another man and I pulled them apart.

The closest pissior was the Men's Room at the Subway station. Not the best in the world, far from the cleanest, a place of grease and grime and porno graffiti and boys of all hues waving erections at whoever came in.

My only hope was to make it to my apartment. I was lucky. I made to the building and my wife buzzed me in.

The elevator was out of order. Frustrated once again I took a deep breath and all two hundred ten pounds of me ran up six flights of stairs. On the way up I nearly ran over the exotic Syrian woman who owned the apartments. She looked at me like I was crazy.

My wife met me at the door with a What have you done now?

I leapfrogged her, dropped my trousers and made it to the throne in time. I had never known such relief.

Somehow I managed to break my sunglasses.

I still had to go to work.

I told my boss the reason I was late was I attended early morning service, a euphemism for making love.

He suggested I attend the Midnight Service if I wanted to go on working for the company.

When I told my wife she said she didn't care, she was moving. The winters were too cold, she wanted to live some place warmer, preferably in a house with a yard. I could come or stay, all the same to her.

It took me two months before I got on with Conquest Inc. first in L.A. then Houston. My wife liked the name because there was no comma between Conquest and Inc., a sign the company was not run of the mill. She said I should fit right in.

I was assigned to Contracts. I started as a trainee and retired as Senior V. P. Analyst.

Bomb from HR

Notice to all concerned:

The core knowledged as opposed to the specialized knowledged are to be outsourced. Information regarding Originators and Syndicators will be forthcoming.

I had been with the company I don't know how many years and yet I didn't know if I were core knowledged or specialized knowledged, an Originator or a Syndicator. I figured no matter core knowledged, orginator, either way a Friday of the Long Knives was coming and I was prime.

A young associate asked me to have lunch with him and a Young Turk from HR. I was older than both of them put together.

I mentioned the notice. YT said, "Layoffs are in-teg-ral to business. We are now playing on new playing fields."

I disliked him immediately. I said, "You've had experience on various playing fields?"

He said, "I didn't say that. What I said was if redundancy comes the best thing the furloughed can do is see it as a new opportunity. Things have a way of working out. After all the riffed will receive the best possible package. If I didn't believe that I wouldn't be here."

When we got back YT said, "Don't forget the motivational seminar this afternoon. Not for everybody, just the select and the borderline. Mucho worthwhile."

The summons to attend was on my desk. I read the summons and wondered which one I was, select or borderline.

Wouldn't be long before I and the world knew for sure.

Two Shrinks, male and female, who were full-blown awesome,

were made even more awesome by the PowerPoint display: Conquest Inc. is a Phat Company, Pretty, Hot & Tempting, On the Cutting Edge (To think I didn't know what Phat meant until that moment.)

Think, Visualize, See

Prestige Power

Turbo Economics

FOCUS ON SUCCESS

Productivity = Profit

Increased Productivity = Increased Profits

Be a Rainmaker

Decade of the Brain

I added my own stream of conscious PowerPoint:

Life Affirming Co-Dependency Negativity Inner Child

Primal Scream Dysfunctional

Loser loser loser

Repressed memories of the variously abused Who's fucking (I had a fondness for the word) who?

Induced pleasure, peace of mind to avoid pain

Cost cutting Full Time Employment We pay for performance (Right)

You are on a need to know basis. If we tell you we'll have to kill you.

I returned in time to hear the male shrink say, "This is the Decade of the Brain. This phat company is dedicated to saving brains so they may be used in new ways."

I laughed and was sorry I did. The male shrink made a note. I was no longer borderline.

The seminar ended when the female shrink looked my way and said in her best ever nurturing voice, "Individual conferences will be scheduled as needed."

I still had a job but no telling how much longer.

The Head of Human Resources, otherwise known as our very own oxymoron, dropped by. "Mark your calendar. Lunch tomorrow at one. Dan will join us. Should be fun. You've met Dan, haven't you?"

I said, "You mean Dan, our erstwhile President and CEO. Of course I've met him. I agree lunch with Dan should be fun."

As he left our very own oxymoron said, "By the way, congratulations, it isn't everyman who's pissed in the company fountain and lived to tell about it."

With the idea I might soon be dead or at least be out of work, I didn't see the giant Turkey Buzzard stuffing himself with road kill at the entrance to my subdivision. I tried to miss him by running up over the curb. I didn't.

Three five year old boys laughed and made exaggerated motions of jacking off. I missed them but I almost hit a constable as I backed into the street.

For a minute I thought she was going to make me clean up the mess. She didn't but she followed me home. She got out of car with the swagger cops have. She, as cops say, approached the subject vehicle, mine, with her right hand resting lightly on her pistol.

She stood with the sun behind her. I had to squint to see her. She said, "I could give you a ticket. You live here?"

I said "Yes" and pushed the garage door opener. My wife's Acura was gone. I said, "My wife is running errands."

She said, "Busy day?"

I nodded and she patted me on my shoulder like bullies do. "Glad to see you have your seat belt on. Keep it on when you drive. The thing is to watch where you drive" then as officers of the law say, she exited the cul-de-sac.

I pulled into the empty garage. I wondered where she was and when she'd be back.

Inside no note on the refrigerator, no message on the answering machine.

I got a Michelob and went to my study. No e-mail.

Housman with his, "Malt does more than Milton can do to justify the ways of God to man" was about right.

It was a good time to bring my resume up-to-date, but I kept thinking about last Saturday Night.

My wife and Melanie from across the street had gone dancing. Melanie's big as saucers eyes were all lit up. My wife looked a little like what have I let myself in for.

I offered to be the designated driver. The two were quick to remind they weren't in the fifth grade. Off they went in Melanie's SUV.

One, two, two-thirty, no SUV. I thought of calling 911.

I felt silly but I had to do something. I jumped in my wife's Acura and took off on what turned out to be a four hundred mile round trip. No one could stay with me, one stretch I blew a Thunderbird away.

I got back at six-thirty. My wife was sitting in her skivvies drinking coffee.

I said, "I've been worried sick."

She said, "You've been worried sick? Why'd you take my Acura?"

"Simple. No one can pass it if you don't want them to."

She said, "I know. I would've been home sooner but Melanie fell in love."

"Did she? Who with?"

"A tall, handsome, suave, sophisticated, black doctor looking for oral sex. I declined."

"Melanie gave head in a parking lot?"

"I didn't say that. The only thing I can say is she and the doctor left together. The doctor said he was more than willing to take her home. Melanie said for me to wait.

So, I waited. I didn't ask what she did while I waited."

"The question is what did you do?"

My wife took a sip of her coffee. "I told you I waited." She smiled, "I haven't had a night like last night since college." She finished her coffee. "By the way where did you go?"

"No place in particular. Here and there."

She knew how to pick her spots. "How would you like a quickie for breakfast?"

That was then, this was now.

If I were terminated (shots firing, the sound of execution), riffed, furloughed, made redundant, even the best of packages, mowing yards, raking leaves, scouring highways for junk, wouldn't be enough.

The thought hit me like an axe. If I were riffed, my wife would be better off if I were dead. With money from my insurance, my 401k, plus any pension, plus savings, plus severance my wife—or should I say widow—would be able to pay off the house, her car (she could sell mine), the credit cards and have something left.

With her brains and energy and a serviceable pudendum she would be all right.

My high maintenance daughter would have to stop saving souls in China and come home.

I said "What the hell" and went outside hoping I could will my wife home.

Melanie in a sexy something was at her mailbox. We waved. I felt strange knowing what I did about her.

The phone rang. Goddamn telemarketer.

I had another Michelob. Being in love and drunk and mad wasn't going to be easy.

I was a million miles away when my wife shook me. "Join me in a shower?"

I didn't bother to ask where she'd been and she didn't volunteer.

I told her about the e-mail, the seminar, The Decade of the Brain and the lunch.

She soaped my back and slapped me on my butt, "Some people will do anything for a free lunch."

I didn't expect fear to take the shape it did. I said, "I've failed you."

She became warm and smiled like she did when we were first in love. She said, "The prospect of wealth didn't win me. The wildness did. It's been missing."

In the midst of loving I said, "I could run guns to the rebels."

She said, "You can do that later. Go to sleep. Remember lunch."

There are times life is good and there is a God. Lunch was cancelled. I may have been borderline but I wasn't riffed.

I was sent to the company shrink. He took one look. "I don't give tests. I don't do therapy. I do salvage work." He scratched his head and gave me the once over. "Don't I know you? Didn't you get kicked out of the University?"

I didn't answer. He said, "Never mind. Go back to work. Consider yourself salved."

I gave him my best Elvis impersonation from deep in my bowels, "Thank you very much."

Life with a Managing Director

Normally I didn't work with the Director In Charge of New Business. I usually worked with the Managing Director in Charge of Service.

Alone, Buddha, as the M.D. in charge of New Business, liked to be called, was pleasant enough. His business card read:

Buddha, Harbinger of the New Nirvana, Wealth
Director in Charge of New Business

He had started out as family rich young man, but through skilful use of family and connections and hard work he had become a corpulent middle-aged man of wealth. He'd learned early on he didn't know diddly-squat about the business, but as I said, he worked hard, and whatever else you could say he was a natural born salesman. His best quality was he'd learned early on to depend on experts for help.

We'd worked on a few projects together and had gotten the accounts. He asked me to sit in on a meeting with a new prospect. I didn't want to. I'd met the prospect a couple of times and I didn't like him. He was a venture capitalist, an entrepreneur, owner of conglomerates, a force that never let you forget he was rich and you weren't. After talking to him for a minute I was glad I wasn't rich.

Someone had printed "GREED. I'm rich, he's not, they're not, you're not" on the chalk board.

Buddha's first thought was of me. "You do that?"

"No sir."

"Erase it and print this in its place: If God didn't need the Rich He wouldn't have made the Rich."

I'd no sooner finished than prospect arrived.

The two men shook hands.

Prospect, "'If God didn't need the Rich He wouldn't have made the Rich.' Love it. Make a great bumper sticker."

Buddha, "Thanks. It's been too long. Thanks for coming."

Prospect, "Thanks for inviting me. I assume you're going to the Prayer Breakfast."

Buddha, "At fifty thou a plate how could I not go."

Prospect, "The President told me he expects to be there."

Buddha, "To return to why we're here. I thought instead of the usual presentation I'd tell you something about us. That way you will know what we're about."

"Fine. Shoot."

Buddha gave his all. "Conquest Inc. is a hundred and one. We didn't get to where we are by luck. We believe hard work makes for profit and we believe in profit. Our goal is to help our clients gather efficiencies so they may cut costs and increase profits. As our clients profit, we profit." A small laugh, "When that happens, we Managing Directors get a bonus."

My immediate thought: Where's my bonus?

"Each Managing Director is a working officer of the company and serves as an Account Executive. Despite what our competitors say Managing Director doesn't mean Managing Dictator."

I knew several employees who would disagree, given the chance.

"Our workforce consists of the best and brightest minds. Conquest Inc. provides an ambiance conducive to good work. No one can match it. No other firm offers the same comfort of long term security, the chance to grow, to work with sophisticated clients, with leading world markets. Like virtue our work in many ways, is its own reward.

"We are spare but not anorexic. We do not gorge ourselves in good times then practice bulimia when times are hard.

"Conquest Inc. is paternalism at its best. We fire only for cause. The borderline know who they are. Long ago we discovered useless anger is counterproductive."

I never understood why management felt it was necessary to rub our noses in it in front of prospects or clients. I once asked a Senior Managing Director why. He said as far he I knew it was a legacy handed down from slave owners.

Whatever the reason, prospects and clients ate it up.

Despite all, the work was interesting, the action intense, the people bright, even when arrogant.

Buddha put on his It's-in-the-bag smile.

"We are solid, we are traditional, yet innovative. We think outside the box. We spread our horizons but not our butts."

Neither Buddha's or Prospect's ass would have fit in a number 4 washtub.

Buddha smiled, "We would appreciate your business."

That was all. The two hugged.

Buddha pulled me aside. "I want you to do something for me. Follow us."

I did as ordered and followed the duo to Buddha's office.

Buddha said, "Welcome to my office. Mi casa es no your castle."

Prospect laughed.

Buddha said, "Make yourself comfortable, I am." He took his jacket off, his shirt and tie, his shoes but not his socks then settled back in his recliner.

Prospect said, "I'm fine, the way I am, but you can get naked if it'd make you feel better."

Buddha said, "Remember when we would hunt whitewing and afterwards go into Juarez and play Silver Streak?"

Prospect said, "You always claimed you won. The truth is you never got past the second girl."

Buddha said, "The Good Old Days."

The conversation shifted to talk about bourbon and farms, hunting and fishing, the best places to vacation, the world's best brothels, French, German, English, Japanese, Thai.

Buddha said, "Nothing would be better for this country right now than a good, first class depression."

Prospect said, "Amen" and asked me what I thought.

I said a first class depression might do the country good, but it wouldn't do me any good. They laughed.

Prospect said, "I'd love to stay and talk about old times but I have to get on down the road. Good seeing you."

Buddha said, "Good seeing you" and fell asleep.

Prospect said, without irony, "I can truthfully say I've not known many men like that man. Now if you'll get my parking ticket validated and show me out, I'll be forever grateful."

I said, "Would you like to see the office."

"Whatever you say."

Prospect knew most of the Managing Directors. It was fun watching the M.D.'s do a business genuflect.

When we got to his limo, the man thanked me and asked me if I'd ever played Silver Streak.

I said, "Can't say I have."

"You put six beds in a circle, each with a girl. Whoever completes the circle wins."

I said, "I've never played Silver Streak and I've never been to the Prayer Breakfast."

Prospect said, "You still have something to look forward to, don't you?"

I said, "A man always needs something to look forward to."

The man laughed then we shook hands. "You can tell Buddha he's got an order for the business. I'll send a confirming fax when I get back to the office. Nice meeting you."

I said, "Thank you for the order. Nice meeting you.

Before you go, I'd appreciate your signing this. It takes the place of the fax until we get your fax. You and Conquest Inc. are officially in bed together."

Like the smart business man he was he read it before he signed it. I'd brought an extra copy just in case. He complimented me on my foresight.

His chauffeur with the aid of a platinum blonde with a movie star face, long legs and natural tits, helped Prospect into his bed on wheels.

The chauffeur looked at the blonde and said to me in a voice that was pure sotto voce, "His secretary eats her young."

As I watched the limo pulled away, the man and Ms. Platinum opened the sun roof and stood up. The man jabbed the air with his fists, "Remember, Wealth's the ticket."

Ms. Platinum waved.

When I got back to Buddha's office, he opened his eyes, jabbed the air with his fist and said, "Wealth's the ticket" and returned to his narcolepsy.

Buddha, Prospect and Ms. Platinum were enough to make me almost a communist.

I left a note on Buddha's computer. "Prospect said the next time he sees you he'd like a drink of that bourbon you keep hidden. He also said you are some kind of salesman. You must be. We got the order without telling the man what we could do for him."

Somehow I'd made it to Middle Management where I actually had some power.

I was hopping mad by the time I got back to my office.

It didn't help my secretary was on the phone in violation of the company rule, no personal phone calls unless it was an emergency.

She was saying, "So you have a need. What can I do? That sounds like fun. I'll be there."

I had to say something to her but what. She had long hair, a sultry voice, a nice face, a good neck, small breasts and a well-shaped ass.

I decided to be magnanimous. I slammed my office door shut. I needed to talk to my Paranoia. We'd gotten the account too easily, we could lose it just as easily and whose fault would it be? Three guesses. Mine and mine and mine alone.

My Paranoia in a rare display of common sense said "Believe what you want. But remember the man isn't a blind hog hunting for acorns; he's an intelligent man who has a reason for everything he does. In this case it might be a favor owed, in-laws, long lost cousins, the same offshore banker, a shared courtesan, college lovers, even incriminating pictures, bribery, theft of the family jewels, dope, traffic in illegals."

I said, "Actually the reason is simple, the deal is a good for both. Conquest Inc. is shrewd enough not to get into major crime."

Paranoia said, "Believe what you want."

The problem was What was I to believe?

As if on cue my secretary came in without knocking. "A bunch of folks want to see you. Curly Locks has called three times."

Although I was responsible for some employees Curly Locks wasn't one.

Curly Locks, thirty-five, born to wealth, per current rumor had had his navel inlaid with diamonds.

No matter the man barged in without so much as Hi, how are you, how's the family, how they hangin.

He said, "We didn't get the account we were working on. Why? You screwed up the Due Diligence clause, the Force Majeure clause, as well as the insurance and indemnity provisions."

The way he put his hands on his hips reminded me of my mother of the way she put her hands on her hips when she scolded me.

"You not only screwed up, you screwed up royally."

I said, "It's not the first time someone around here screwed up royally. It won't be the last."

Curly Locks nailed me. "It could be yours."

I said, "I don't believe my ears. The man's a goddamn crook. Conquest doesn't need his business."

He said, "That's not your call."

I said, "Somebody had to make it."

"Such decisions are Management's."

"Want me to tell...."

Curly Locks said, "Management already knows" and left. It was going to take a miracle to save me.

My secretary stuck her head in, "That's one."

Next was our file clerk. Normally I wouldn't have been her supervisor but management had decided it might be good if I learned how to supervise people.

She was an unnaturally thin, twenty-five year old single-mother with not much education but with a brain and a good attitude.

She wasn't happy. "I've just come from my annual review with HR."

"How'd it go?"

"It went well. She said my job is my raise."

"She said your job is your raise?"

"Yes."

I said, "There is a new company policy that says no raises for the foreseeable future. I thought I beat the deadline."

She said, "You may have, but I didn't."

I didn't tell her I'd had one raise in seven years.

She said, "Do you understand what I told you? The woman said my job is my raise. It's up to me to make of my job what I can. I'm responsible for what happens to me. I said like if I'm killed in an earthquake, burned to a crisp in a fire. The female prick said Yes. I said I used to work for the Post Office. Going postal is nothing new to me."

I said, "You said that?"
"No, but I thought it."
I said, "Not a bad thought."
She said, "Not a bad thought. But no raise."
I said, "Sorry."
She said, "Sorry is right."
I thought that'll teach me.
My secretary said, "Next."

Strictly speaking 'Next' man didn't fall within my supervisory authority.

Fact is I didn't know 'Next' but I'd known his father, an up-front, what you see is what you get oilman-rancher, a sharp as hell mean as hell rock hard old bastard you could depend on to be just that. I wandered how far from the tree the apple had fallen.

Next said, "You do this?"

Will the individual who scrawled 'I will give head to men with often hard on' on the wall above the urinals in the Men's Room please contact Human Resources.

I said, "I don't do graffiti."

He said, "I see."

I said, "I hear you wiped out one of Charley's best companies."

"True. I was big time. The Networks flew in special crews to show me being awarded The Distinguished Cross and a battlefield commission. Everything was going as planned until at the last moment I declined both. My timing couldn't have been better. General Wheeler was pissed off no end."

I said, "I hear the General still is. So tell me, why are you here?"

He said, "I have a question. When two men make love, which one is the homosexual?"

I said, "You tell me."

He said, "Me tell you? How would I know?"

I said, "I don't know. Experience?"

He said, "This is getting us nowhere. I'm leaving but I'll be back.

Next time we'll talk about pleasure and pain and various types of violence." He left smiling.

My secretary said, "I don't believe it. You made him laugh."

I said, "It's all in knowing how."

My secretary had no fear, "You see his eyes? They were like marbles. Speaking of eyes, your beady-eyed friend from Executive is on his way down. You might have a look at these files. I found them in your In Box. Some are potty trained, some are old enough to shave, some have beards. Survival time, Boss."

I felt like the man who'd lost his blindfold before he was shot.

Beady-eyed came in without knocking.

I said, "Doesn't anybody bother to knock anymore?"

He said, "Good to see you're hard at it."

I said, "What you see is what you get."

He said, "I might say the same thing. You game?"

"I'm game."

"In that case I have some good news and some bad news. The good news, Monday morning Conquest is starting a New Quality Control Program. The bad news, I'm going to be your auditor."

I didn't even say Shit. All I said was, "Lucky me."

He grinned. "A word of advice. Monday morning, be ready to kiss ass. Mine."

"Look forward to it."

Like a warning a gull and a pigeon lit on the ledge outside my window at the same time. The gull ate the pigeon.

No doubt about it my ass was in a sling. I made a list of things to do if and when.

Live under the viaduct, heed the call of the movies, move to The Border, run a whorehouse, teach illiterates to read, sell food stamps on the black market, go into the printing business, print fake Green Cards, drivers licenses, Social Security Cards, birth certificates.

Raise money for fake charities, hire out as a world class rabble-rouser, write religious tracts, get rich, channel back to Joseph, get his side of the story, sell photo copies of dollar bills to addicts so they can cheat dealers and run the risk of getting shot, hire out to make obscene phone calls, spam friends, wander the world, become a hermit in the desert.

Capture an island, invade the U.S., win the lottery, become so dangerous thousands quake at the sight of me, be the best goddamned comic ever, so sophisticated everyone would pee down their legs, become a pimp, an assassin, a fucking burden to the world.

I looked at my list and thought I should have been so funny when I was doing standup.

Ms. Missionary coughed. "Sorry. Your secretary said to go right in. So here I am."

I said, "That fucking woman is going to be the death of me yet."

Ms. Missionary played her hole card. "I could have you fired for that. All I have to do is tell Mr. B."

I said, "I wasn't talking to you, I was talking to myself."

She smiled, "I forgive you this time."

Once she'd been a good woman to work with, but she'd turned into a smart ass narrow minded woman.

She smart assed me with words. "Mr. B. asked me to remind you that ten days have passed since he asked you to tell him what you thought of e-mail. I've never known Mr. B. to be this patient. What am I to tell him? I have to tell him something."

"Tell him you talked to me and I said, Scratch that. Tell him he'll have the memo Monday."

"No lie?"

"No lie."

She dropped a fax and bent over to pick it up. She had an ass like a Gala Apple.

I said "Is that for me?"

"You mean the fax? It's about you. I was going to tell you, but Mr. B. kept it."

I said, "Remember when you called me a Preterit? I didn't know what the word meant."

Ms. Missionary said, "Passed over by God, left to eternal death."

I said, "I looked it up."

She said, "You provoked me. There's nothing worse than a man who knows he should believe but doesn't. See you Monday morning. You will have Mr. B.'s memo."

"Yes."

I wondered how anyone so religious could have such a sexy walk.

My secretary said, "What is it with you two?"

I said, "Whatever it was I just killed it."

My secretary smiled one of her cute but meaningful smiles, "Speaking of killing, Curly Locks wants you to call him."

C.L.'s voice oozed with an actor's charm. "You were right. The man was and is a crook. We have no business doing business with him. He stiffed us. Mr. B. says no more. I should have known better. I apologize."

I hung up so happy I went to see Mr. B.

"I understand you have a fax for me."

"It's not for you. I can tell you without having to kill you the lender thinks the work you did on the Argentine project is better than state of the art."

I almost peed all over myself before I got to the Men's Room. The guy at the urinal next to mine tried to sneak a peak.

I reared back like I was riding a wild horse. "Whoa, Big Fellow, whoa!"

Monday was going to be a day to remember. I had an audit that could determine my fate with the company. I had an overdue memo, best to get it done or reserve a pallet in a city parking lot under the Viaduct.

Still, I'd had a good day. Curly Locks had eaten crow. I'd had a nice fantasy, a left handed compliment from the boss and a good pee. The weekend was good. I got nookied twice and took two naps.

Monday. Work intense as always. Did we lose the account? Did we get the order? Was I about to be fired? Why in view of the edict No raises were two men hired at half again what I made, plus a bonus to do the same work.

Management's answer: We have our reasons for what we do.

I learned then, Humor is not always kind.

Missionary came by.

I said, "I know I said 'First thing, Monday', but I don't have Mr. B.'s memo."

She said, "Like I've been trying to tell you. God exists and He cares. Mr. B. is out of town."

If only Executive wouldn't show. But he did. We went in a small conference room not unlike a psychiatric ward.

He took off his coat, turned off his cell phone so his wife couldn't interrupt us. He read every line in every file like he was walking through a minefield.

When he finished he sat back and looked at me. "Your handwriting could be better. You're slow at times. Other times you're faster than the quick and the dead. Your hunches are right for the most part. Not as many mistakes as I expected. Not as many out and out screw ups."

I said, "Thank you."

"The amount of work surprised me. Your attitude suggests a lighter load. I don't get you. You know the lay of the land around here. Why fight it? Take Thompson. Six months ago, a hard worker among many hard workers. Then he got the message. What is he now? A Managing Director, part and parcel of the system."

I said, "A goody-goody turned ass kisser."

"I'll do you a favor. I'll pretend I didn't hear that." He looked at his watch. "Later than I thought."

I said, "Time flies when you're having fun."

He gave me a half-ass dirty look. "You'll be receiving an evaluation with suggestions. Read them. Pay attention to them. Conquest Inc. has been at this longer than you've been alive. A loose cannon is scary."

I said, "You should write a book. *Hegemony in the Office.*"

"That's the last thing I'm going to pretend I didn't hear."

There it was, a sudden end to friendship and I had survived the day. I turned to thoughts of the memo.

Once I got into it, it flowed like wine.

E-mail: Better than grenades, sturdier than barricades, more elusive than spies, perfect for a yes here, a no there, a truth here, a white lie, a pure lie, distortion, misinformation, disinformation (a term I disliked), spin, an altered contract, raises for everyone, commerce, lives rearranged.

Perfect for passive aggression, a time waster without equal, a network for dalliances, love letters, chain letters, hate mail.

E-mail: Provoker of new peace

E-mail: Provoker of wars

E-mail: Ever changing, ever changeable

E-mail: The orderly transfer of chaos

E-mail: The connector

E-mail: The purveyor of Everything

God bless, you, E-mail, bring it down, bring it all down, it won't hurt, after a while.

I liked my memo so much I read it at supper.

Geek, aka my son-in-law, arched an eyebrow but kept quiet. He'd never rocked a boat in his life.

My daughter said, "Why must you always make everyone uncomfortable."

I said, "A small price to pay for eloquence and wisdom."

My wife said, "Whether eloquence or wisdom, it is sure to get you fired."

I said, "I see your point" and decided to kiss ass.

The finished product may be the most fatuous piece of writing I've ever done. My only defense is it had to be done.

The idea behind e-mail is the quick exchange of accurate information that depends on eternal vigilance.

Left to itself e-mail may be pirated, spammed, infected with worms and viruses that change daily. Conquest Inc. has the best encryption devices money can buy, but even those protections may be corrupted. Hackers are no dummies and they are everywhere.

All e-mail is to be printed and filed with the correct file. If no file exists create one.

A copy of each outgoing e-mail is to be circulated with the day's spinach.

No e-mail chain letters are permitted and no pornography.

E-mail will be monitored by Human Resources. Abusers may be terminated for cause.

A change of address and password is necessary from time to time.

E-mail is only a tool. Professionalism is the key.

Our Computer people, Human Resources and Department Heads are available for help.

Remember, Be on Guard.

I got it to Mr. B. on time.

He gave it his supreme compliment. He signed it and circulated it without change.

I felt ashamed afterwards. My secretary said she could see why.

The e-mail memo didn't do much for morale. Neither did the

fact that when someone left, they weren't replaced, workloads increased, people were pissed off.

Strangely Productivity increased. Conquest Inc. was making more money than ever. Yet the rumor of another Friday of the Long Knives persisted. Our chief competitors had streamlined their work forces, so why not Monkey see, Monkey do?

I believed the question to be an understandable reaction since our species has a natural attraction for the dour.

I believed another axe was about to fall when chaos or serendipity, blind luck or divine intervention, saved my ass. Our man in Colombia ran away with a great deal of our money, our intellectual property and the trophy wife of a drug overlord. I was given a chance to go up the ladder or slide back, Colombia was to report to me.

Our Colombian expert in recovery was a polite, gracious, apparently kind man, who did not shy from thoughts of murder, "Sometimes thieves and adulterers think what they've stolen is rightfully theirs. They become reluctant and recalcitrant, more difficult to deal with, more difficult to catch. In addition to my usual fee, it will cost more to rent a truck to run them over."

Until that moment I'd never thought the man and his concubina might have to be killed.

I said, "I don't want them dead."

He said, "I don't want them dead but doing business in Columbia sometimes has additional costs. What do you want me to do?"

"Catch them, get our money and our intellectual property back."

"Consider it done."

Within two weeks our man had recovered our money and intellectual property. I didn't ask how and I didn't ask what happened to the lovers and he didn't offer.

I wasn't especially proud of myself. Mr. B. said, "It's like war. You do what you can. You don't think about it afterwards."

When I went to work for Conquest, I promised not to give up comedy completely. Two dead lovers in Colombia wasn't the highest form of comedy but it gave me an idea:

L.A. Noir

The room was spacious and comfortable with a view of Catalina which was beautiful when the weather was clear and the weather was clear. In spite of the weather a local astrologist had predicted a tsunami. Meteorologists laughed.

The voice at the door was insistent, "Maintenance."

I went to the door with pistol in hand and opened it.

The potbellied Chinaman with lips as tight as bob wire was no maintenance man. He was about to learn his stairway had let good fortune out and bad fortune in, his mirrors were hung crooked, his shade trees were on the wrong side of the house and had grown too tall. No more make money, lose money, make money.

I said I was sorry for his misfortune then popped him and left him for the maids.

Miss Redhead on the elevator pushed against me with everything she had. She was soft and firm in the right places. I licked my eyebrows. She came. I licked them again.

The elevator opened onto the lobby. The four blacks with Mac 10's didn't think I saw them. I watched them cross the lobby in skirmish formation. Not a pimp or a dealer among them. Each a professional. I treated them the same way I did the Chinaman.

Ko-Jo stepped from behind a marble column. "When word of this gets around people are going to think you're a racist. How are you, my lover?"

"Better now that you're here."

We hugged.

I said, "The last time I saw you four Crips were doing their best to make me a permanent part of Olympic. When they saw you they vanished. There wasn't much else to do but make love."

She said, "First time see you, no make love. Me frightened young mother on her way to Seoul to show off infant son. You on way to Seattle. You take baby, help find seat. Fold stroller, put in overhead."

"Ko-jo, please can the Charlie Chan."

She said, "I swore I'd never forget you."

"You fed me baby crackers all the way to Seattle. Which reminds me, I'm hungry."

The next thing I knew we were at The Cupboard Home of the best Sea Cucumbers in L.A.

Ko-Jo smiled and grabbed me by the crotch and squeezed. My s.c. jumped. She said, "Nice."

She had ham and eggs. I had a stack of buckwheat pancakes, five eggs, eight links, a half-pound of bacon, six biscuits, a jar of strawberry jam, a pitcher of orange juice and two jugs of coffee.

Ko-Jo said, "Your belly looks like Brazil the way it hangs over your belt. Which reminds me, I'm moving into Brazil, Radio, TV, Music, games, entertainment of all kinds, plus banks and power plants. I need you to run things. You will be more than wealthy. What do you think?"

I said, "I don't know. Brazil to me is the Amazon going dry, disappearing rain forests, killing and kidnapping, street children a plague, AIDS, the pull of music and dark pussy. As DeGaulle said, 'Brazil is not a serious country.'"

Ko-Jo said, "The country has changed. Brazil is a serious country. I need your answer by the time we get back to the hotel."

I said, "I hope the maids have cleaned up the mess."

We didn't pay. Ko-Jo put the cashier with big tits to sleep with a swift move invisible to the unpracticed eye.

I said, "You haven't lost the touch."

Ko-Jo was naked by the time we hit the back seat. Her breasts were the color and shape of small yams. Her lower pumpkin mouth beckoned. I took a chance on not many teeth.

We made love twice and were back at the hotel.

She sighed "Well?"

"I pass."

"Too bad."

The scene was fucking Byzantine.

I waved as the limo pulled away.

I started up the steps to the hotel. The Doorman went into a karate stance.

A piece of walking grime, the sentimental would say he had the look of spiritual intelligence, put a hand out. I took one look and said, "Take a bath. Get a job."

The advice didn't faze spiritual intelligence. He pointed to a man as bloated as a dead pig. "There by the Grace of God goes Charley, your brother."

I gave my bother's keeper, Charley and the doorman candy silver dollars laced with the smell of almonds. They toppled like fallen idols.

The astrologist was right about the tsunami. The building yawed. Glass shattered. The street turned into a roiling river. I was sucked under. I figured the moment of lasting contentment had come.

I woke up on Malibu Beach to the sounds of a righteous riot. I prayed for an extended fuck. I must've prayed to the deity. My prayer went unanswered.

The cold Pacific read me my rights and rolled over me.

I was swept out on a monumental riptide. In no time I was overcome with eternal contentment.

It wasn't long before everyone in the office was talking about *L.A. Noir*. Ms. Missionary didn't waste any time going through my desk looking for a copy.

My ex friend from Executive said, "The man's pissed. Can't help you this time."

HR was up in arms. I was a waste of time and money. I was sent back to the shrink who said, "I've already done you. Get back to work."

That wasn't enough for Mr. B. He waved his copy of my masterpiece in my face and said in that wonderful way he had, so everyone could hear, "You do this?"

"Yes."

He threw his copy of *L.A. Noir* at me. "That is not what we pay you for. We pay you to do your job. So do it."

He had no sooner left than I began to write

My New Career

Me, Executive V.P. Ed Wilson, Rayette, his Niece-Secretary with the Big Hair and Sybil, Director of Human Resources, stood in President and CEO Abbott's office watching the man himself toss a glass paperweight globe in the air and catch it.

He said, "Remember the song 'He has the whole world in his hands?' Reminds me of me."

Wilson said, "It's supposed to be about God."

The man himself smiled variation twenty of his mean smile, "That's why I like it."

Abbott put the paperweight down. "Ed, if you and your sweetmeat want to make love on company time, you need to find another company."

It was a tough way to lose a twenty-year old Niece-Secretary with a mouth designed for rock stars. Ed turned purple and grabbed his dick like a little boy.

Sweetmeat said, "Uncle Ed, go ahead and pee in your pants. I'll tell Aunt Ellen what happened. She'll understand."

Ed turned a darker shade of purple.

Sweetmeat spit her gum out and looked at Abbott. "I'll see you in court."

Abbott's smile was as tight as a piece of wire. "Do that. See what twenty-six unexcused absences in six months will get you."

"Plenty. I was harassed to the point I couldn't do my work. I had to seek professional help."

Abbott said, "Is that right, Ed? We pay a girl to fuck and then harass her to the point she can't? To where she has to seek professional help?"

Ed let go of his dick, wet his pants and had a heart attack. He was dead before the paramedics arrived.

Abbott showed his sorrow at the loss of his best friend the way those without shame do. "Ed Wilson was not only our Executive Vice President he was my best friend.

His loss is a lesson for us all. Ed came close, but no one is indispensable."

Rayette, no longer Sweetmeat, smiled and shook her head, "And people say you aren't worth killing. Shows you how wrong people can be."

The Man Himself grinned. "Sybil, call security."

Security appeared in the guise of three guards who ushered Rayette-Sweetmeat out. Sybil said later they reminded her of The Three Shepherds.

Abbott said, "That wasn't so hard, was it?"

Sybil said, "No sir."

Abbott, the Man Himself said, "That young woman killed my best friend. How am I supposed to tell his family?"

I said, "Why not let Rayette tell them. She was his niece."

The man took his time looking at me. "I don't know you, but I assume you work here. Yet, every time I see you you're doing nothing but standing around jawing. Nothing personal but I want you out of here by Friday."

The man's time was coming. I didn't know when. All I knew was I'd be there.

A weary Sybil showed me to her office and shut the door behind me. "Your not-exactly-golden parachute will be ready Friday."

"Whoopee!"

"Better than Free Fall."

I said, "I'd like to knock Abbott on his ass."

"He won't be here the rest of the week."

"Call me when he gets back."

Sybil grinned. "How would you like a one time job of more pleasant work? The pay is fifteen hundred, but there'd be other compensations."

"Is this conversation being monitored for quality control?"

"Don't you trust me?"

"What do I have to do, kill Abbott?"

"Yes." She bit a fingernail to the quick. "Ouch, I need to get to Nails Supreme."

I watched while she sucked on the finger.

She looked up embarrassed, "I suppose you know I'm Abbott's biweekly fuck."

I said, "I didn't know how often."

"You wouldn't know it but Abbott's good in bed. Of course that's neither here nor there." She sucked on the finger again. "The man was right about one thing. No one is indispensable. No one. Not even Himself. You were in Special Forces?"

"Wouldn't do any good to deny it."

"Ever, uh"

"There was no Abbott."

"You have a problem?"

"None I can't handle."

"My son in high school is in the arms trade. He can deliver a .22 pistol with silencer and all the ammunition you will ever need by mid morning Friday and not miss his appointment for fellatio."

"Good for him. What about the stipend?"

"What do you say to seven fifty Friday afternoon when you pick up your severance package along with the piece and ammo. The other seven fifty plus tip afterwards."

"My tip?"

"A night with me."

"No thanks, I might fall in love, then what would I be, the new Abbott?"

"You are funny."

"Thank you. When, where?"

"Wednesday night at the Komedy Klub off the Freeway on the way to the beach."

"The Komedy Klub, where women who want to disappear go."

"Not since Abbott took over. Different clientele, different entertainment. Wednesday is First Time Night. The winner gets two fifty."

"A good reason to be there."

"Abbott won't be suspicious. He'll think you need the money."

"Yeah, the money. I'll be a rich man."

"Don't forget the tip if you change your mind. It's worth more than money."

"I won't forget."

"Abbott likes to make love in the trailer behind the club. Shoot him while we're in the act."

"On the rise?"

"Like your style. Be there."

"I'll be there."

"The last thing I need to do is send the cops out looking for you."

I said, "Who's funny now?"

Sybil tightened. "You better be if you want that two-fifty. Now, excuse me. Your package needs my attention."

I left. My first gig and my first contract. All I had to do was be funny and kill a man. 'Nothing personal' would soon have a new meaning for Mr. Abbott, The Man Himself, President, CEO."

The parking lot was empty. The Klub dark.

A topless Sybil was waiting for me. It took a while before I could take my eyes off her breasts.

"The News showed pictures of the smash up on the Freeway. I was afraid you"

"I had a flat, which was bad enough. Remember the song, 'I heard the crash on the highway but I didn't hear anybody pray.' Try changing a tire in the dark in the middle of a wreck on the highway. You'll hear somebody pray."

Sybil smiled. "You're here and that's what counts."

"What about the other seven fifty?"

"Here. Sorry about the two fifty."

"The fault of the gods." The envelope with the seven fifty was nice and plump. I tucked it under my shirt next to the .22.

Sybil said, "I better get back. Abbott's waiting. Give us a minute or two. Have a beer."

Every time Sybil moved, her breasts bobbed up and down like corks on water.

I turned the lights off. It took two minutes to down the beer.

Abbott was too busy to hear me.

Sybil said, "Abbott, look who's here. Mr. Abbott was saying fat women work harder and longer and cheaper, that they are good in bed and give great head and are forever grateful."

Sybil and Abbott were amazing, they didn't miss a beat.

Abbott looked up.

I said, "Nothing Personal" and shot him between the eyes.

Sybil laughed. I decided to forgo the tip.

I reread My New Career and wondered what it'd be like to tell Mr. B. 'Nothing personal.'

I know it sounds crazy but with Columbia behind us the office was quieter, a new spirit of cooperation appeared. People began to talk about how to make things work better. Looking back, the new spirit and the new mood never had a chance.

The air turned electric with talk of poison gas, shootings, cannibalism, lay offs, unemployment without benefits, wives gone mad, AIDS, AIDS, AIDS, AIDS, wars and future wars, illegals, runaways, atomic weapons, the H bomb, terrorists delights, earthquakes, floods, holes in the ozone, global warming, dengue fever, the return of smallpox, anthrax by mail, flesh eating viruses and bacteria, the only signs of hope, a group of terrorists blew themselves up and flowers were blooming in mountains where they'd never grown.

I asked Missionary what she thought. Her eyes glistened, "It's started."

About that time, the mail boy stuck his head in, "Someone just bombed the hell out of the Federal Building in Oklahoma City."

Missionary said, "See."

The next morning.

The voice came in loud and clear. "This is the Head of Human Resources. We have just received a communiqué from an organization calling itself The New Jihad that two bombs have been planted in our building the purpose of which according to the communiqué is to destroy the building and kill everyone in it.

"We have informed the FBI and a team is on the way. In the meantime we will exit the building in an orderly way just as if it were a fire drill. The Fire Marshall on each floor will supervise the exit."

The Fire Marshall on our floor said she had heard Mr. Head Honcho Himself had grabbed his jacket and said, 'I don't know about you all but I'm getting the hell out.' I plan to do the same."

I did my best to see that everyone on our floor exited the premises in an orderly fashion.

Afterwards I checked to see everyone was gone. What I found was one stayed because the boss, who was nowhere to be found, hadn't told him he could leave, another because he didn't believe there was a bomb, another because he had work to do, another because she believed it was God's Will, and one because he believed whatever happened had to be better. One couple stayed behind to make last chance love in the file room.

I wondered if I was supposed to make a list of those who left and those who stayed. I decided not to.

I thought about going up on the roof. The rumor was in the event of an emergency, a helicopter would ferry the Executive Committee to the safety of a Gentleman's Club. I told myself if I played my cards right I'd be able to hitch a ride. Then I might not. I wasn't on the Executive Committee and more importantly I hadn't been invited. The only thing to do was walk down twenty-one flights.

I was lucky. The pretty and the scary, a gaggle of female attorneys from the law firm on the top floor accompanied me. They nodded but went on talking about reruns of "Sex and the City" and "Friends."

Once on the ground there were no Security Guards, no police, no National Guard to tell us what to do or where to go.

Some stood and gawked at the building, forgetting it would be adios if the threat was real. Some headed for the basement in the garage. I headed across the bayou, not because a photographer was taking pictures of a naked woman with heavy breasts and gray pubic hair but because it seemed like a good idea.

The Boss Attorney of the gaggle saw me and smiled.

"I don't understand why would anyone want to blow up a building filled with pussy."

I blushed and got aroused like I did in high school when the Most Beautiful Girl said Hello. The arousal wasn't quite the same but it was nice.

I said, "I don't know, crazy people, zealots, believers (then I lost it) I have a friend who thinks our troubles are caused by females who insist on hot waxing their pubes."

She looked at me like I was crazy but kept her poise. "Interesting. I'd like to hear more but I'm being summoned. I know where you office. I'll call you and we'll do lunch. I need someone to talk to. Bye-bye."

I thought, Yeah.

Word came down, there was no bomb.

I got back to my office just as the Head of HR came by taking names of those who had stayed, those who had returned and those who hadn't.

He saw me and said, "Lucky you."

Things rocked along until everybody got scared about Y2K and the Millennium.

There was much weeping and wailing, people feared computer clocks wouldn't turn, planes would crash, ships at sea collide and sink, in comparison the loss of the Titanic would seem inconsequential, planes would crash, and in cities traffic lights would fail, power would be out on a scale never imagined, cars would careen and crash, elevators drop, fires burn out of control, people die by the thousands.

The prospect for chaos, a New Dark Age, was upon us.

Mucho dinero was spent. Lawyers got richer. Missionary said, "Don't be surprised if Armageddon comes."

I said I'll try not to be.

People thought I was crazy when I told them I believed the Millennium was already here.

While people waited for catastrophe with baited breath, my wife and I, in a once in a lifetime moment, climaxed as one with the birth of so-called New Millennium.

Work was as before until 911.

The New Business Committee Meeting was late in getting started. No one had bothered to turn on the TV. So a flock of us were watching Missionary make sure each of us had a pencil and tablet, a folder with a copy of the agenda along with last year's results and this year's goals, plus a list of prospects while the caterer was busy making sure we had enough to eat and drink.

The future had never looked brighter. Pax Americana, Globalization, Empire, The Decade of the Brain, the death of History (I for one had never thought of Communism as History), no more 8.0s on the Richter scale of international politics, only a ripple now and then, but nothing the U.S. couldn't handle.

We had no idea what was happening, until the mail boy turned on the TV. We saw the jets strike the Twin Towers, we saw the devastation, the fires, the dust and debris, people jumping to their deaths, the collapse of each tower, the miracle of people walking out alive, helping each other, the bravery of the firemen and the police.

The conference room was overcome by profound silence. A silence followed by spontaneous rage. Kill the rag heads, nuke the sand fleas, give the fanatics what they want death, shoot them before they shoot us, Give them what they want, Kill them, Send them to Hell.

The words weren't much. The rage was. If anyone had even hinted we brought it on ourselves, he would have been trampled.

Two days later I was given a Lapel Flag as a reminder of those who died in the Towers, those who sacrificed their lives by crashing United Flight 93, those ready to fight the terror.

It wasn't long before the Lapel Flag came to mean report suspicious behavior, to believe dissent treason.

My secretary said she feared for me.

Time passed. My wife asked if I'd written the piece on the op-ed page about Iraq and the declining quality of our lives.

I told her No but as a white American Male of mixed Western European Ancestry with a touch of Apache I was proud to be a secularist, a bastard son of the Great Satan.

I told her not to worry we had plenty of duct tape.

It looked like my idea of connecting longings and feelings was falling apart. I told myself the thing was not to quit.

Inkling

The only thing I knew about the man was he was a Managing Director. He smiled and said he had something to show me, did I mind?

What he had was a picture of his wife of thirty-eight years on Safari in Kenya. She was dressed like a white hunter and was standing over a man with the biggest penis I'd ever want to see.

A note read, "Having a wonderful time. As you can see the hunting is great, more than I ever imagined. I'll not be coming back."

I had no idea why he'd chosen to tell me. Perhaps he felt more comfortable with someone he didn't know but recognized.

I said, "Sorry."

He said, "What would you do if your wife were to suddenly vamoose?"

I said, "I don't know."

He said, "You might want to think about it."

The thought of my wife suddenly leaving hurt. But there it was. Something was wrong. It hadn't been anytime since she'd told me twice she was sick and tired of me. I'd put it down to passing anger.

I needed to talk to someone who knew me but didn't work for Conquest Inc. I knew just the person. We decided to meet at an out of the way cocina where we used to meet for lunch. The search for another love was on.

I got to the cocina first and sat where I could see her when she arrived. Arrive she did, tall and as lanky as her brand new Lexus.

Kathy looked good in her designer jeans. If I didn't know any better I would have sworn her cowboy boots were made out of human skin, She smiled and greeted me with "Sorry I'm late" and the obligatory social kiss on the cheek. I had hoped for a kiss on the lips.

I asked how she was, how she'd been.

She said, "Wonderful."

I said, "You seem to be doing very well."

She said "I am. Ron and I are divorced. Business couldn't be any better. Remember what a mousy thing I was when I worked for you. I've changed. I am no longer peter whipped. I travel when I can. Just this year I've been to Nevis, the Keys, Ireland and Paris. I think Paris is the most beautiful city in the world. Don't you agree?"

What could I say but "It goes without saying."

She said, "Tell me, what can I do for you?"

"I'm not sure. Remember the time we were rolling around naked on your bed and you thought you heard your husband. You locked yourself in the bathroom and said you wouldn't come out until I left."

She said, "I was scared."

"So was I. I got dressed as fast as I could and ran. I turned the corner just as Ron pulled into the driveway."

She said, "I never told you how happy Ron was to find the table set. But enough of the past how's the world treating you?"

I said, "Fine, just fine." And I was. I had fallen in love again with her soft neighlike laughter.

She said, "That's good to hear. I'm thinking of buying some property in Cabo. What do you think about Cabo?"

"To tell the truth I've never been there." Right then what I wanted to do more than anything was rest my head on her small bosom and have her stroke me and tell me she loved me.

She said, "My ex tells me at one time you did pretty good standup."

"I wasn't bad." I relaxed and did "A Woman's Private Moment," and "Why God Wet her Panties."

That ended the lunch. She grabbed the ticket and said, "I never want to see or hear from you ever again. God is going to get you."

The tamales were good.

I made my second call.

"May I please speak to Ice Pants?"

The voice said, "You have the wrong number and hung up."

I waited for Ice Pants to call. She agreed to meet me for lunch. She showed up in a glistening green suit with a blouse that showed enough cleavage to make me want to run a finger around the rim of the valley.

She said, "I want you to do me a favor. When you call, if I don't answer the phone, don't ask to speak to Ice Pants. My fires aren't out. Men put off their shoes before my bush."

"Forgive me. I promise it'll never happen again."

"What's on your mind?"

"My wife is getting ready to bolt."

"What'd you do?"

"Nothing."

"Yeah, right. Tell me something, you trying to get in my pants?"

I said, "It's not a bad idea." I started to ask if I'd have to take a number but didn't.

She said, "I love you but I'm not going to sleep with you."

I said, "You love me but you aren't going to sleep with me?"

She said, "It's the best I can do."

I went silly. I told her about the picture of the woman on safari, about my wife's being sick and tired of me. Then I made a mistake, I told her about Woman with two Vibrators, Man with Pump, God was Upset.

She said, "God is going to get you."

I said, "I just as soon She didn't."

She said, "You're terrible. By the way your barn door is open."

I looked down.

I said, "At least the mule isn't out." I zipped up. But didn't give up.

Second date.

She said, "Sorry I'm late."

"Sokay. You know you have a sweet face and really big boobs."

"Thanks for the compliment. The face just happened. I've had the boobs since I was nine."

"Mind if I have a look? Areolas are a hobby of mine. All I need is thirty seconds. Okay?"

"No. To change the subject, remember Sally?"

I said, "Yes."

"Remember how bad she wanted to get married? Well, she got married all right, to a wife beater. He beats her up, says he's sorry, then gives her a pearl necklace. You know what a pearl necklace is?"

I said, "I thought I did."

"Sally's husband does. He comes on Sally's breasts, Sally the good wife she is thanks him for the pearl necklace."

I said, "You sure know how to destroy a mood."

She said, "You might say that. He offered to give me one. He'll not do that again." She smiled, "I tell you that so you won't get your hopes up. Which reminds me I'm seeing someone. He's older but not nearly as old as you."

"Hardly anyone is. Tell me about him."

Ice Pant's face lit up. "Let's see. He's been divorced five times, so he's not looking to get married, which makes two of us. Oh, yes. He's a fantastic lover. Where no one else could he taught me to come. And not just once."

"The hell you say."

"The hell I say. Excuse me, I have to pee. Order me a Caesar's Salad with grilled chicken."

Neither of us said another word until after I paid the check.

She said, "By the way, how is your wife?"

I said, "Loyal, trustworthy and true."

Third date.

She was in a hurry. "I have a lot to do. I'm getting married and moving to Paris. Texas."

"I thought he'd sworn off marriage."

"Not the same guy."

"What's this one like?"

"He asked my father for permission to marry me and for his blessing."

"Must be serious."

"It is. He is. I am. I love him."

"I wish you well."

"I know you do. You know, if you weren't so slow on the uptake, I might be marrying you. Remember when we wanted to go to this Chinese restaurant but it rained so hard we couldn't get out of the car. I wanted you to kiss me so much. But you didn't."

"I was afraid."

She said, "I thought of grabbing you and kissing you."

"But you didn't."

"I was afraid."

I said, "Such is life. Oh well, it's been."

She said, "Give me a high five."

I gave her what was probably the worst high five ever.

She said, "At least you tried. Give me a hug."

I wanted to grab her and give her the kiss I should have. Instead I gave her a hug that was more than the social hug where people pretend their bodies touch. Ours touched.

We stayed that way until she looked up at me and patted me on the back. "You hug better than you high five. I have to go. Wish me well. And don't worry, you'll find someone."

I found someone, not that kind of someone but someone from the office. She was twenty-eight, black by today's standards, if she hadn't used the makeup she did people would have thought she was white.

I couldn't look at her without getting all screwed up about age and race and sex.

A romance novelist might have called that day at the elevators a fateful day. She looked me up and down. "Well, if it isn't one of the slaveholders."

"Not me. I'm not an M.D."

"You could have fooled me. You look like a slave trading son of a bitch. It's nice to know you're not."

"Thanks. You know 'He's Nothing but a slave trading son of a bitch' would make a good title for a C&W song."

She laughed and showed her movie star teeth. I wished she'd bite me, which in its own way sounded country.

I said, "Why don't we go to lunch some place where we can talk?"

She said, "I don't screw for a free meal."

I said, "Sounds like song to me."

We became songwriters. Titles came easy.

"I'm Not a Free Meal."

"No Money No Love No Fun."

"Nails on the Highway of Life" sounded so good we figured it was already a song.

"You're the Rain that Breaks my Drought, the Storm that Floods my Soul."

"I Never Knew My Body Could Make a Sound Like That."

"I Told Yew to Stay in the Truck."

"I'm Only a Commode to Yew."

"Jump My Bones? Yew Wish."

We argued about if we dropped too many g's or used too many Yews.

It didn't matter. I loved the lingo.

We didn't sell a thing. We fired one last shot, "Flat Out Pissed Off At Yew."

She found a better career. She sent me an e-mail, "Leavin' on the Night Train."

I left a message on her voice mail, "Yew Can Always
Sleep on the Sofa of My Heart."

The fact we didn't make it hurt. The money we lost had nothing to do with the hurt. What hurt was we failed to shed even a little light. Our corner was no brighter than before.

I didn't know what I was going to do until Serendipity in the form of a voice on the phone said, "Remember me? The attorney from the bomb scare."

"We were going to do lunch. You were going to call. I thought you'd died. What can I do for you?"

"It's not so much what you can do for me as what I can do for you. If you're interested, meet me at noon by the elevators on the Plaza level."

I couldn't help it, I said, "Today?"

She said, "What do you think?"

She was young, not twenties young or thirties young but forties young with an easygoing maturity.

She said, "I thought we'd pick up a couple of submarines and go to the Hideaway."

"Fine by me."

The Hideaway was a two room condo. The living room-dining room with a Plasma TV, a CD player, wet bar, a full bath and a kitchen compete with refrigerator, two built in ovens, a stovetop, a double sink, an electric dishwasher, a pantry, with enough room left over for a breakfast nook, and a half bath was downstairs. The washer and dryer were in the attached garage.

Upstairs was more Spartan, a double bed, a vanity with a mirror that faced the bed, one closet, a cooler with beer and a tub that sat on a dais. A work space with desk, a P.C. with printer and fax.

I said, "Where's the phone?"

She said, "No land phone. I prefer my cell phone."

I said, "Erotic pictures on the walls but no mirrored ceiling? Why?"

"I could tell you I'm shy. A friend who aspires to be my lover has offered to install a mirror in exchange for beer and pussy. I haven't made up my mind. If you're interested the beer's in the fridge. The pussy is, well, me. While you're making up your mind this pussy is going to take her clothes off."

She stood there grinning like a proud naked six year old girl.

"What'd you think? Do I have enough pubic hair?"

"Yes."

She said, "It's red because of nature. The hair on my head is platinum blonde because of my husband."

She put a green striped beach towel on the bed and lay back. "You are going to take your clothes off?"

"I thought we would talk."

"We don't do anything if you don't take your clothes off, not even talk."

It took me a while.

"My, look at you. Kiss me."

"Nice. My husband never French kisses me. I like it."

She patted the towel. I sat. She said. "Now, let's talk. A little personal history so you won't have to ask. I got married the day after I got my B.A. I was a virgin, so was my husband. He wanted it that way, not that we didn't do our share of heavy petting. Were you a virgin?"

"No."

"Was your wife?"

"No."

"You, uh?"

"Her first? As far as I know."

"As far as you know?"

"It's unimportant."

She rolled on the bed like a cat.

"My husband is an oilman, generous to a fault. He put me through law school. We make love religiously. Give me another kiss."

She said, "That was better than the first. Let me catch my breath. That's even better. So you won't have to ask, my husband as generous and loving as he is tends to over control. Rather than fight I take lovers."

I said, "An interesting form of revenge."

She said, "I think so. I've had two. The first was John Wayne Engineer, my husband's best friend. I call him John Wayne Engineer because he thinks he looks like John Wayne and he is an engineer."

I said, "Sounds reasonable to me."

She said "It's something to make love to your husband then screw his best friend."

"I can imagine."

"Can you imagine this? John Wayne Engineer and I are no longer lovers. My second lover was a Professor of Art at the University. He called himself Art Bloc. He was a toe sucker. You a toe sucker?"

"I tried it, once was enough. Do you all?

"No. Like John Wayne Engineer he made the mistake of telling me he loved me. The only man who can tell me he loves me is my husband. Remember that and remember this, I'll never tell you I love you. I'll never tell anyone anything. I expect you to do the same.

"This isn't an affair. It isn't a relationship. It is what is. One more thing, I'm not interested in your personal history. Understand?"

I said, "Do I have to sign anything?"

"All you have to do is talk when I want you to and make love when I want you to, in the fashion I want you to. Don't worry I don't have any STD's."

I said, "Neither do I."

She said, "You don't have to worry about my getting pregnant. After my second miscarriage, they took the crib but left the playpen."

I swooped down and kissed her breasts.

She said, "God, I love that. You'll like this. I come in four minutes."

It took me three.

She said, "Next time I'll be in control. Don't forget."

"I won't."

She hadn't come but there was going to be a next time.

Yes!

The trouble with next time was she wanted to show off her new metallic red Corvette. She raced every kid in sight. Once she had it up to one thirty-four. We didn't make it to the Hideaway.

We stopped for frozen yogurt instead. She was splendid in her orange and brown pantsuit with earrings and bracelets and pendants and rings worth I don't know how much. She got a kick out of the way the kid behind the counter stared.

On the way back to the office I grabbed a breast.

She laughed and pinched my crotch.

That was it. She let me out before she parked.

She called that afternoon. "It was nice not going to bed. I wanted to see how you would handle it. You handled it well. There's nothing to worry about."

I couldn't help but worry.

The next time we went straight to the Hideaway and made love. I did more than asked. I complimented myself.

She said, "My influence. Incidentally, my partners think you're gay."

I said, "What do you think?"

She said, "How many men have you had?"

I said, "I didn't think you were interested in my personal history."

"I made the rules, I can break them."

"In that case, no more than my share."

"How many women?"

"None until you."

She laughed and traced the outline of my face with a finger. "Recently my husband invited my long lost cousin to dinner. That night they agreed to a Joint Venture to drill off Singapore. My cousin wants my husband to be President and CEO. If he accepts we'll have to move."

"Interesting."

"That's not all that's interesting. After dinner my cousin followed me to the kitchen and kissed me."

"You kiss him back?"

"Not exactly."

"Not exactly? What does that mean?"

"Not exactly means what it says."

"Not exactly means what it says. Is this it?"

"No. The first time I saw you naked I didn't see any hope. I was wrong. You're a great fit. You're funny, you're kind, you take instruction well. Makes all the difference."

She lay back and I swooped down and kissed both breasts.

She said, "Have I told you I love it when you do that?"

"No."

She laughed and wrapped her legs around me.

I was content to lay there in her grip. She said, "I have something else to tell you. Two weeks ago, John Wayne Engineer begged me to sleep with him."

"It's your body."

She said, "I don't need that."

"Sorry."

"It wasn't as pleasurable as I remembered. I told him there was someone else. You know what the egotistical bastard said? 'There's no one but you, darling.' When I told him I wasn't talking about him he looked surprised. I thought you'd like that."

"I do. You ever make love to Hubby, JWE, Art Bloc and me, the four of us, the same day?"

"I give you a compliment and that's what you say to me?"

"Sorry, it was a jealous thought."

"Yes, it was."

I lay there afraid.

She smiled and said, "Look at that. Where did he come from?"

She pulled me over on her. "I like the feel of your heaviness on me."

We made love a third time.

My secretary said, "That must've been some lunch."

I'd just hung up from talking to my wife when my secretary said, "You have a call waiting."

"Who is it?"

"Some woman."

Some woman was right. She said, "I need to see you. Meet me at the Hideaway after work."

She was naked when I got there. Her fondness for the cryptic and impromptu had taken a new turn.

We made love on the floor. Her feminine vigor became masculine, intense, desperate.

Instead of tickling, teasing, pleasant afterplay she pushed me in a chair and straddled me.

"This is our last time. My husband has accepted the JV offer. We leave Sunday."

I said, "We both knew it had to end."

She said, "That is the most out and out romantic thing you've ever said to me."

"That isn't all. I have something for you. You can think of it as a This Is the End Present."

"You are romantic."

"I've had it for sometime, but I've been afraid to give it to you."

She smiled, then said softly, "Do you have anything else romantic to say to me?"

"Only that, You're great!"

"That's enough. What is the This Is the End Present?"

"A Diary of Love."

"Yours?"

"I wrote it but it's for you."

"Read it to me."

"It's meant for your eyes. You might want to read it in private."

"Since this is our last time together, I'd like you to read it to me. Please."

I said, "It's in my coat."

She said, "Where's your coat?

"Over there on the floor."

"Go get it. Please."

I said, "Save my place."

She said, "You are nasty."

I cleared my throat.

She said, "Before you begin, tell me, this isn't going to take long. I have to be home by midnight. I have an appointment to carouse with my husband and my cousin."

I said, "At the same time?" I'd hoped it would come out funny but it didn't.

She laughed anyway.

I said, "It begins 'Dearest.' The last time I began a letter with 'Dearest' I was fourteen. I'd met a girl at church camp. A flurry of prayers was followed by a flurry of kisses and after camp a flurry of letters, letters like…,"

She said, "Let me guess. 'I've never known anyone like you, our love will last forever. I love you I love you I love you I always will. Write soon, Sealed with a kiss.'"

She smiled, "Well? Do I know fourteen year old girls or not?"

I said, "I've often wondered what the postman thought when he saw her red lip prints all over the envelope."

She said, "He probably didn't even notice."

"One day no letter. She quit writing," I snapped my fingers, "just like that. I never did find out why."

She said, "You want to know why? She was fourteen."

"True." I took a breath and gave her what I hoped was my best stage smile, 'Dearest, Forgive me for breaking your rule, I'm not saying this because I want to get you in bed, I'm saying this because I love you.

"'You are my Olympia, my Naked Maja, more beautiful than Modigliani's Mistress, more ravishing than the naked Georgia O'Keefe.

"'Shakespeare once wrote something like Wonderful! Wonderful! Oh Wonderful! I think Pretty, oh Pretty, how Pretty!

"'I don't know who first thought it but Desire does transform. Desire transformed me. I never thought I'd feel this way about anyone."

She interrupted, "Should I tell your wife or do you want to?"

I said, "Now, who's nasty?"

She said, "I'm not a sentimental person."

I said, "There's more. 'I take my time, I kiss your hair, your eyes. I swoop down on your nipples. I tease your belly button, it's better without the silver ring. I linger over your movable feast, you guide me to other fancies.

"'I stretch out on you, you stroke my back, I flip you over and munch on your buttocks like I would a baby's.

"'I am sorry I am not a toe sucker.

"'You are a bromeliad, an amaryllis, an Iris, a Blood Lily, you are full flowering and transforming.

"'You're bittersweet pain, You're love. I wallow in your tyrannies, your surprising mercies.

"'You turned sex into love. I have never made love so well, never loved so.

"'You are greater than Eve.

"'I will love you after the hammer falls.' That's it."

She said, "Nice. Did you keep a copy?"

I lied, "No."

She tore it in two and lit. We watched it flame then become ashes in a wastebasket.

She said, "So much for evidence" then looked at me, "I didn't do that to hurt you."

"You didn't?"

"Let me finish. I'm not a sentimental person but I never want to be forced to explain you to my husband, to God, or anybody. Our times together mean too much, even if we never did bathe together."

I said, "I have the time."

She said, "In that case, my husband and cousin can wait."

It was like I'd never had a bath.

She dried me off and pushed me on my back. "You don't deserve this."

The goodbye kiss lingered.

She said, "I love my husband. Be careful driving home."

I wish I could say the last time I saw her she was standing naked in the doorway, waving Goodbye.

But I can't. The last time I saw her she had her back to me.

I took to bringing my lunch. It wasn't long before my secretary said, "I know it's none of my business, but."

I said, "It is none of your business but what?"

"You've quit going to lunch."

"I have a lot to do."

"How much yogurt can you eat? How many peanut butter and jelly sandwiches? How many apples? How much bottled water can you drink?"

"I'm trying to lose twenty pounds."

She said, "What is it kids used to say?"

"Bull corn?"

She said, "That's it. Bull corn! A man would never say he's trying to lose twenty pounds. Only a woman would. A man would either lose twenty pounds or gain twenty pounds."

She sat on the edge my desk crossed her legs and said in a husky voice, "I know I'm a secretary but I'm a good listener. I'm also a good lay."

So, everybody wanted to know. I said, "I appreciate the offer. I think we both better get back to work."

An invitation to suicide came during dinner. My wife said, "Do you have something to tell me?"

"No."

"Is there someone else?"

"No. Why? Somebody say something?"

"Some psychiatrists think an unfaithful husband makes love with his wife more often than a faithful husband. Case in point. The past two months we've made love like eighteen-year-old newlyweds."

I said, "Really? I hadn't noticed. Have you been unfaithful?"

"That's it, change the subject. I'm not the one who's been unfaithful."

I said, "Neither have I."

My wife's concern with my fidelity reminded me of My wife's concern with my fidelity reminded me of missed opportunities.

The young English War Bride left alone in a new house in a new subdivision. I was seventeen and trying to sell magazine subscriptions. She invited me in and gave me a coke. She said she was sorry she couldn't write a check. Her husband wouldn't let her. All she had was a dollar. Was that enough?

The girl in high school who in one year took on the starting backfield of our football team, the starting five on our basketball team, the two captains of our track team, as well as the captain of the baseball team. She came to me and said it was time for someone from the boy's debate team. Wasn't I on the Boy's Debate team? I called her a bitch. She chose my debate partner.

The black lady of the night in Galveston. She picked my pocket.

The latina at the end of the block who liked to stand in her bedroom window and rub her belly as I walked by.

We were newlyweds. My best friend Fred and his date were our first dinner guests. After dinner Fred suggested a foursome. His date was game. My wife wasn't. A threesome was out of the question.

The Christian Lesbian for Jesus.

The self styled nympho who kept saying she would but never did.

The girl with the big ass who chose another.

The woman in Denver who dangled a leg and said, "You don't know what you're missing."

The woman taking her blood pressure on a machine that didn't work sat so I could see up her skirt. She looked at me.

"The machine says I must be dead. What do you think?"

I said, "She's not dead. I saw her wink."

There were exceptions. The Army nurse called me her little rabbit. I took it to mean I could go several times. She said it meant one time rapid fire.

The blonde who looked like Lana Turner.

The none too happy wife of a drunk friend.

If this were a Victorian Romance the next line would be "Years passed." Years did pass but not enough for me to retire with full benefits. Just when it looked like I was going to be home free Young Turk who was now Middle Aged Turk and the Head of HR offered me the choice between early retirement and, as he put it, taking a chance on the future. I told him I'd think about it."

He said, "Take all the time you need, Like overnight."

When I told my wife she called Young Turk turned Middle

Aged Turk a bastard, the company a bunch of bastards and me a son of a bitch for always being a step different.

I worked hard at finishing my job, my career, in such a way as not to leave a bad taste in anyone's mouth. A digression: I also did my best to do my writing as well as trying to perfect a Theory of Everything on the sly.

I wanted to believe Einstein's notion of a Unified Field was true even if it hadn't been proved. I told myself So what? Neither had String Theory.

Last Day

A goodbye brunch of guacamole, tamales, huevos con chorizo, mangoes, beef fajitas, borracho beans, and for dessert fried Mexican ice cream.

A gift card from Missionary, a goodbye French kiss from my secretary. But no take care of yourself from on high, No, we had our moments, from Missionary, no stay in touch, no come see us from Curly Locks, my executive ex-friend or Mr. B.

I managed to get everything on my desk into the right file. My desk had never looked so clean.

I had to do something. I couldn't just sit there and look at my desk. PBS was running something called This I Believe. I borrowed, I say borrowed I had no intention of returning it, a pad from my secretary. I had a pen. I did my own version of This I Believe only I called it The Accumulated Thoughts of a Working Class Idiot.

The corporate world is not Democracy.

Which comes first, rights or the bottom line?

Absolutes, despite their convenience, are a hindrance.

Absolutes cause more trouble than digital. (I had no idea what that meant when I wrote it. I still don't.)

Absolutes are a dictator's best friend.

Beware of cutting costs, of trimming the fat, of cutting back, of there is no I in team, of God loves the ennobling power of poverty. You thought the idea poverty ennobles was dead, didn't you?

You want to hear something funny, really funny, the rich would rather eat dog food than come up with a way to redistribute the wealth.

You may have heard God committed suicide because of the unintended consequences that resulted from His/Her creation.

God, if He or She exists, has not and would not commit suicide because of any unintended consequence. With God there are only unintended consequences.

God did not intend for the bougainvillea to be a bougainvillea, the prickly pear to be prickly pear, the palm tree to be a palm tree, the cocoa leaf to be a cocoa leaf, Mama Coca to be Mama Coca, God did not intend for The Gran Remedio to be The Gran Remedio God did not intend for munificent irony to be munificent irony, God did not intend to be a Humorist too big for any one religion, but He-She-It is. A new definition of the Trinity arrived at by an unintended consequence.

I wasn't sure what to do with the list. I came close to tearing it up. For a minute I believed I was about to be defeated.

Before I left I papered the Coffee Room Bulletin Board with my notes. Which was nice but it wasn't enough. I sent one last e-mail:

To Whom It May Concern,
Please note the following thoughts.

I signed it: WHO YOU CALLING A FOOL?

I sent a copy to This I Believe.

To jump ahead in the story I never heard from PBS.

The night when I got home, my wife said, "What now?"

I said, "Us."

She said, "Us? Jesus Christ!"

"Us? Jesus Christ!" was no sooner out of her mouth than I was hit with:

Some marriages are wildly passionate from the git-go, surviving youth, middle age, old age, senility, until death separates, then no more abuse, no yelling, no taunting, no sarcasm, no browbeating, no more flashes of light from a slap, no more you brought it on yourself, you made me do it, you didn't give me an out, no more I hate you, no more so what if I did sleep with him, no more so what if I slept with her, no more I'm going, no more once I'm out that door I'm gone, I'll not be back, no more you're not human, no more overflowing in public, no more three day disappearing acts, no more wild-making-up-I-love you sex.

Some marriages are wildly passionate in a different way until death, filled with expressions of love, holding hands, walking arm in arm, sudden kisses, sneaking into the woods making love at 30,

40, 50, 60, 70, a quick feel in public, on the elevator, in church, at weddings, at a funeral for a friend, a former lover, making love on the kitchen table, the floor, in the shower, making love in the front yard at three in the morning on a dare, in the rain.

Some marriages are passionate in a still different way, the romance of ancient newlyweds, face to face, head to head, body to body, soul to soul, thinking not of what was, what's to come, but what is.

Later we had a sumptuous dinner at my dinner club, lump crabmeat, chateaubriand, asparagus, Baked Alaska.

When we got home we were as nervous as summer lightning. We read, we talked, we made love, still neither of us could sleep.

My wife said, "Listen, someone's in the house."

I said, "I don't hear anything."

She said, "I do. I don't know why you don't. You deaf?"

I said, "I do now."

I kept a bat and a flashlight by the bed for such emergencies. I grabbed them and told my wife not to move I'd be right back.

My wife didn't help when she said, "Be careful."

Fortunately I didn't find anybody, I thought for sure I'd find my daughter Courtney and her current husband Geek. I say current, actually Geek was her first, it's that I never expected it to last.

No matter I still heard laughter.

I peeked through the curtains on the front windows. A naked Amazon of a girl was laughing and dancing and rolling around on our driveway.

I told my wife to call 911.

She said, "We might want to think about it, what with the new neighbors and all."

"New neighbors?"

"They moved in, I think it was two weeks ago. I met them this afternoon before you got home. The father works for an oil company. The mother is the number one secretary for a bank president. The Amazon is their only child, I say child, she is thirteen."

I said, "Thirteen?" and opened the door and smiled. The Amazon stood and waved and returned the smile. She didn't look thirteen. I stood there until she waved and left.

My wife said, "What do you think?"

I said, "Lucky driveway."

She poked me.

The more I thought about the girl the more I became comfortable naked. I discovered a new sexual vigor without the aid of Viagra and began to parade around the house naked. I told my wife not having to strip saved time.

She said, "Take it outside."

Which I did at three the next morning. I had no idea the female Constable who had followed me home would be the one to see me.

Sitting handcuffed and naked in the no-way-out backseat of her patrol car was not my idea of fun. Neither was being threatened with a few nights in the psychiatric ward.

What convinced the Justice of the Peace, who left a comfortable bed to see what was going on, I wasn't on the prowl, that I wasn't insane, was that at no time did I have an erection.

The Deputy Constable gave me a ride home. Once in a while she would look at me and smile.

The upshot was I was fined a hundred fifty dollars and told I could either ride shotgun for the Neighborhood Watch two nights a week for the next four weeks or go to jail.

The first thing I had to do was buy a weapon. The clerk suggested a Liberator, a shotgun as short and nasty as a cottonmouth, great for shooting rabbits and would-be burglars.

The first thing my wife said when she saw the Liberator was she hoped I'd remember we were to love our enemies and return good for evil.

I said I'd remember.

Six of us crammed into the Honda. The driver cradled an AK47 on his lap. His wife who sat between us always wore a tight fitting sweater and carried an Army .45. Whenever we went over a speed bump her breasts brushed against me and the .45 poked me in the ribs.

Her breasts were nice, the pistol scary. She whispered she couldn't wait for the chance to blow someone away.

A guy in the back seat was very proud of his sawed off shotgun. He'd stroke it and say, "Imagine the look on the bastard's face when he hears the last thing on earth he'll ever hear."

The man next to him said the high point of his life was bayoneting

Chinese in Korea and pitching them over his shoulder like so much hay.

The guy next to him looked ashamed. "All I've ever done is wish my boss were a grease spot."

I shivered. What would I do if my nonviolent gene overcame my Attila the Hun gene, if my serotonin level didn't drop when I saw a burglary in process, a kid stealing a car, a man beating his wife in the front yard, a wife returning the favor?

I needn't have worried. Night after night what we found was a neighborhood at sleep. My tour of duty ended.

It wasn't long before the driver's wife blew her husband away because he was there.

The guy who wished his boss were a grease spot was killed when he went looking for sex and crack, as the song goes, in all the wrong places.

The man who'd enjoyed bayoneting Chinese soldiers had a mental breakdown.

The man with the sawed off shotgun thought his son was a burglar.

I gave up walking in the nude.

My wife took to shooting the Liberator, just in case.

She liked the sound and the feel of the weapon so much she took a turn riding with The Neighborhood Watch.

The Amazon ran off. She sent me a card from Seattle.

After Retirement

Sometimes our married life was a contest to see who could irritate the other the most.

My wife wouldn't admit it but she was the winner hands down. She had a skillfulness to die for. She knew I was not to be disturbed when I was online.

"This won't take a moment. All I want to know is, Are you planning to kill me?"

I said, "Funny you should ask. Just last week you said if you found the Liberator you'd liberate yourself."

"I said no such thing. I said if I found the Liberator I'd never divorce you."

"You also said you might take a baseball bat to me when I was asleep."

"True. I also said I'd run you over, push you off a cliff, drown you in the bathtub. I even prayed you'd pass out in the garage with the engine running. When you didn't I quit believing in the efficacy of prayer."

"Is that all?"

"Here's my favorite. I would screw you silly then smother you." She smiled, "At the time I meant what I said."

"Why?"

"As if you don't know. You hounded me no end, day after day, night after night, blaming me for God knows what. You loved to humiliate me in front of my friends. You packed my bags and put them in the yard. You have no idea how humiliating it is to come home and find your bags in the front yard. You got so bad I didn't dislike you I hated you. The strange thing was the thought of my killing you didn't seem to bother you."

"Why should it? I knew you were thinking of killing me long before you told me."

"How can that be?"

"When we made love which wasn't very often, I was no sooner in than you moved your legs and I was out, not accidentally."

"You never said a word."

"I didn't see any reason to. I figured if you wanted to kill me you'd find a way."

"I probably shouldn't tell you this but there was a time I longed to see your brains scattered about in pools of blood."

I said, "And yet, here we are, no worse for wear."

She said, "Ever wonder why a bad time got better? I have."

I didn't say anything.

She took her time then said, "Maybe it's because even though we're not forgive and forget Christians, we are forgive and forget people. Then, maybe it's because we not only forgive and forget we love."

I tried not to sound too wise, "Love can be as good a reason as any to kill."

She said, "So I'm told. I hereby kill you because I love you. Isn't that wonderful, just wonderful."

I said, "Makes you wonder how much wonderful a marriage can stand?"

She gave me a mischievous sexy grin, "I hope it's not too late to find out."

Trying to find out was a series of unexpected pleasures. As Don Ameche once said in a movie whose title I can't remember, "Things change."

While the unexpected pleasures removed the threat of my immediate death, wonderful didn't exactly solve all of my problems.

When my wife was at her Mac she did not want to be disturbed. Nothing, nothing else mattered.

She taped a sign on her door: This is a Sanctuary. Knock then wait for permission to enter.

One day I didn't wait.

She said, "Can't you read?"

I said, "We need to talk"

She said, "Later. I'm busy."

"I said we need to talk."

"I told you later I was busy."

"I don't mean later. I mean now."

She said, "Now as in right now?"

I said, "Right now, I'm not in the mood for humor."

She said, "Right now, I'm in the middle of something."

I said, "Aren't we all?"

She said, "What I'm saying is, Now's not a good time."

I said, "It's never a good time with you."

She made a big deal of turning off her Mac. "What's so important it can't wait?"

"I had lunch with Fred yesterday."

She said, "Our Fred?"

"The one and the same."

"How is he?"

"He has brain cancer. He's a dead man."

"I'm sorry. I'd forgotten how close the three of us were."

I said, "So had I."

She said, "The next time you talk to him tell him I'm sorry."

I said, "I doubt I'll be talking to him again."

"Oh?"

"He said he was your first, that you all slept together before we were married. I gather more than once."

I waited for her to say something. She didn't. She went back to her Mac.

I said, "Well?"

"Well what?"

"Fred remembered times, places, everything."

"That was the time we decided to date others to prove our love for each other. Fred was my other love, my OL. Who was yours?"

"I didn't have one."

"You didn't have an OL?"

"No."

"Fred was a passing moment, he didn't mean anything, he was nothing more than a lark. Look, I married you. I love you. Courtney is your flesh and blood. It's not like I committed adultery. I'm sorry if that's not enough. Excuse me, I have to finish this."

I didn't hit her. I've often wondered why.

I went on a kind of a strike. I didn't shave for three days. I'd never grown a beard. A lot of men my age had, one even went so far as to boast He and God were twins.

Like the wicked stepmother in Snow White I asked my mirror if I should grow a beard. The answer came back, "You didn't come here to talk about growing a beard. You came here to talk about Fred and your wife. You want to book a Major Pity Party."

I didn't argue. I said, "The thought of Fred in my wife hurts."

"Why, it was years ago."

"We were engaged. He was my best friend."

"Remember Hidden Spring?"

"Not the same. Hidden Spring was her idea."

"I see. In your wife's defense sleeping with Fred seemed to be a good idea. At the time it wasn't adultery. It was a happening, no harm no foul. You don't want to talk about adultery, do you? If you don't, I'll put 'Good Boy' by your name."

I had enough of my reflection. I said, "Goddamn, you."

My reflection said, "Until you can do better than Goddamn you, I suggest you pull your socks up and get on with your life."

My wife said, "Were you talking to yourself?"

"Actually I was having a conversation with my mirror."

"What's your mirror have to say these days?"

"Nothing new. The usual pull my socks up and get on with it."

She said, "Are you all right?"

I said, "I'm not sure. Sometimes I think I'm losing it."

She said, "Aren't we all?"

I said, "I suppose so. Take the mall the other day. While you were shopping, I decided to walk the mall. This thirty-year-old kid practically ran over me. He gave me a look of you had your chance, old man, get out of the way. If I'd had a gun I'd have shot him. His wife did what she could to make it better. She apologized for him then ate him out. You know what he said?"

"Let me guess. 'What'd I do?'"

"Right. The son of a bitch."

"Look on the bright side. You got another card from the Amazon today. She's pregnant. I was thinking we might send her some money. Is that okay with you?"

"We have any?"

"Not much but some."

"I never thought I'd feel this way but girls with their tall, blonde, great bodies, the stories of high school blowjob parties, their confidence the world is theirs today make me feel out of the loop, that the world has passed me by."

My wife said, "Young boys make me feel the same way. Hell, isn't it?"

I laughed.

She said, "I don't know if this will help, but I'm going to bed. Coming?"

The thought hit me. Can it be this woman, my wife, cares for me, loves me? Or is it just a moment?

"Well?"

I said, "Coming."

She said "Wonderful" like there was some doubt.

The New Way

My wife had always put my medicines and vitamins out in the morning. Out of the blue she not only stopped putting my medicines and vitamins out she stopped cooking.

She would take off and be gone for hours without saying where she was going and when she'd be back. When I'd ask where she'd been and what she'd done, if she had a good time, if she got done what she wanted, she'd say, "You don't know, do you?" Sometimes she added, "You don't know much, do you?"

Finally it got to where I had to say something. The best I came up with was, "What's going on?"

"Didn't I tell you? It's my New Way. Everybody has a New Way, the country has a New Way, the world has a New Way. I have a New Way.

"You should have a New Way. From here on you're to be responsible for your medicines and vitamins. You're going to learn to cook something other than red beans and rice. Until you do it's either eat out or cereal."

"We can't afford to eat out every night or even twice a week."

"Cereal then. Get used to it. As far as being gone for hours, I'm writing a book, How to Make Love to a Seventy-Year-Old Woman."

I said, "You aren't seventy."

She said, "I know. I wanted to give you fair warning."

I said, "Fuck me."

She said, "I intend to. In every sense of the word. Excuse me, I have errands to run. I'll be back in time for dinner."

I said, "Be sure to pick up some bar-be-que."

She said, "What about fried chicken?"

I said, "Fine."

When she got home she didn't have either.

I fixed hamburgers.

Finally we compromised. I would be responsible for my medicines and vitamins. She would do her best to tell me where she was going and when she'd be back, allowing for an hour or more.

She fixed the evening meal three times a week. I fixed it three times.

The seventh we snacked, ordered Chinese or pizza or ate out.

Poet in the Making

Every Sunday the museum had a double feature of so called classic and important movies. This Sunday's double feature was a movie about deSade and a movie about King George The Third.

We decided brunch first, retrospective second.

We were sitting next to French Doors which opened onto the sidewalk with its array of passersby worthy of Ginsberg and Kerouac. A nice, bright not as warm as it looked Sunday noon. I was torn between listening to my wife talk about her childhood and watching the passersby. A few made me fear attack.

It dated my ass indelibly but I was amazed at the numbers and different styles of tattoos: Daggers, swords, killer bees, mean looking roses, knives, babies with beards, pistols, private parts, shotguns, snakes, skulls, swastikas, lightning bolts, miniscule messages, psychedelic abstracts, landscapes that crossed the back and wound over the entire body.

The decorations were rarely pretty. Even the ones of Jesus seemed born out of desperation and defiance. The crosses were menacing. I felt uneasy.

I tried for wit and pith but came up with high-minded old fogy, "Tattoos are the graffiti of a sick body-mind."

My wife gave me an ah-ha smile and said, "That the best you can do?"

I shrugged. I'd done my share of wild and crazy things but never tattooed. Yet, looking around at the various tattoos I yearned for the old soldier-sailor-good-times-drunk blue dragon, ring-tailed lions, hearts joined forever by an arrow, hymns to Mother, tattoos. I missed the naked ladies who shimmied when muscles flexed, the stripper's HATE on her left breast, LOVE on her right and BETTY on her belly.

Not even the sight of young breasts with flowered tendrils could shake me from my mood. I winced at the sight of hardware and jewelry piercing the human body and face, at photographs of bells implanted in the foreskins of erect penises. I said out loud, "The death knell of circumcision."

My wife jumped, "What did you say?"

"Nothing. I was thinking of all the available body paraphernalia. I especially like the diamond in the female nose."

"I would have thought you preferred silver rings in the honey pot." She flicked her tongue at me, "I must have mine done."

"Suit yourself, but I prefer a bone through a nose or a needle through a cheek."

She raised an eyebrow, "I'd like a Bellini."

I ordered a Bellini for her and a why bother café latte for me. The waiter laughed, "A Bellini and a skim milk decaf café latte."

The restaurant was quiet and sustaining, different from weekdays with their noise and excitement, the quick and the dead business lunch, the hope and the aura of slam bang sex.

I watched a Japanese couple feed their baby. When he didn't like something he would smile and open his mouth and let the bad tasting food tumble out.

Just down from them were an aircraft carrier, a battleship and two heavy cruisers. They had held up well despite age and many tours of duty.

At the table next to us a boy of perhaps twenty and a man that reminded me of a Queen Mother from graduate school were having brunch.

I pointed the Queen Mother out to my wife who said, "Queen Mother? You don't know. You can't possibly know."

I said, "You're right, I don't. I can't possibly know. Just like I can't possibly know a Chinaman's a Chinaman."

"Tell me, Mr. Kim, how do you know a Chinaman's a Chinaman?"

I said, "Observation and experience."

She said, "Really. What about that bus boy eating that leftover piece of cake?"

I said, "Mexican."

She said, "Mexican, not Latino, not Hispanic?"

I said, "No. Mexican."

My wife had such a deep seated infection caused by the Political Correct germ I couldn't convince her I was being fair.

Queen Mother was getting into the swing of things. "I enjoyed meeting your parents. I had the feeling your mother liked me but your father didn't."

The boy said, "My father doesn't like anybody."

I had a hard time keeping up with the Queen Mother.

"How's school? Made any new friends? Like the city? I hope you don't give up and leave. You have much to offer. Don't let it go to waste."

The boy cut his eyes at the Queen Mother. I wished he had given the man a get-off-my-back look.

The man ignored the look. "Comfortable with your quarters? Your mother seemed to think they were on the small side. If you decide you need something larger, I can help."

The boy nodded.

The Queen Mother said, "Read any good books? Seen any good movies? Had any impure thoughts? Speaking of which, at the museum, there's a wonderful exhibit of drawings of the male member by males. You might find it interesting."

I fought the urge to say, "Then again he might not."

"How's the food?"

The boy said "Fine. What about my poems?" in a way that was close to the edge.

The man wasn't stupid, he kissed his napkin and said in a voice no longer motherly but kind. "Your poems. Have you read Anne Sexton?"

"No."

He said, "You might want to. Her poems are filled with wildness, wild metaphors, wild images, wild thoughts. You would do well to read her."

As much as Queen Mother pissed me off I wanted to clap, I hadn't seen a performance like his in years. I made up my mind, I would read Anne Sexton. I needed a wild metaphor. I had the kind of thought I had in college:

Tattooing is today's wild metaphor.

I asked my wife if tattoos were poetry.

She said it's a thought and went back to her eggs.

I left my thoughts of tattoos and tattooing in time to hear the boy, "There's the red soil. One poem is a hymn to the soil."

Queen Mother had no shame, she was the queen of condescension. "Forgive me, dear boy, I had no idea you came from the soil."

"Your great grandparents did?"

The boy said, "Yes."

The Queen Mother said, "One of the rules of life and poetry is be wary of the love of the land. Write that down. That is an epigram I just made up."

Queen Mother fanned herself with her napkin. "Don't despair. You have talent. The thing is how to cultivate it. You might like to read my paper, 'Rhythm, Meter and Metaphor.'"

Queen Mother smiled. "There are some things a young poet should remember. Today's good poets write for today's other good poets.

"Be careful of graphic language. Graphic language in small doses may be all right. It can have a certain poetry. But as a general rule graphic language is best left to the lower classes. Believe me, dear boy, the lower classes do exist."

Queen Mother was older than I thought.

The boy went beyond sullen into the sulk of the young.

Time was I was a master of the self made sulk.

The man perhaps fearful he had overdone himself said softly, "I've invited a few friends out to the lake next weekend. Why don't you come and bring your poems? You'd have an audience."

The boy grinned, "An audience. I'd like that."

An audience. Before L.A. and the Bellylaff I once shared an audience. I was Mr. Young Comic standing on a downtown street corner acting silly, doing my best to make people laugh while a black preacher kept saying, "Thank you, Jesus. Thank you, Jesus." That and nothing more.

"Thank you, Jesus" and I made interesting music until a cop told us to move on.

The boy turned from sullen to excited. "What do you think of these titles? 'Stormy Gulf,' 'Moon and Stars," 'Prairie and Sun,' "Pudendum and Phallus?"

I wanted to hear Queen Mother's answer but my wife said, "Time to go. We'll be late as it is. When you drift you drift. I was beginning to think I'd have to go to the museum alone."

I paid the check and said, "I'd like to say one thing to our poet."

"Oh?"

"I'd like to tell him to tell the Fuckoff to Fuck off."

My wife said, "You come with me. We might like to come back."

More tattoos, more body paraphernalia as we waited for the car. I said, "This city could use a good De-tattooing and Removal of Objects Parlor. We'd get rich."

My wife took my arm. "You're great. Once a comic always a comic."

I made it through the movies without complaining. The deSade movie had one good scene of a bare breast.

Listening to Queen Mother wasn't a total loss. I got to thinking about words and expressions for our time:

Homeland Security, beware of Duct tape, hurricanes and your neighbor

The Internet, Web, blog, Home page

Collateral Assets

Coalition of the willing

Target of opportunity

Decapitation Strike 101

Shock and Awe

Moral Awe

Insurgency, talon, blue talon, fuel cells

Cyber crime

Mass hysteria

Pandemic

Chatter

Asperberg's Syndrome genius without social skills without guilt

They do what most of us can't

Like an action movie only real

New Military Humanism

Silent genocide, positive violence

24/7

Hit the ground running

Low hanging fruit

Empowerment

Attrited, Degradation, slowly killing the enemy

Surveillance, Dooced

They cause death then there's the human part

Erectile Dysfunction, Four hour erections, a dream, an ideal, agony, A rush to the E.R. Unintended consequence

Out of the blue, a description of my Theory of Everything: If reason is universal in mankind and sets mankind apart from animals humans should be the same at the core; no need to pay attention to motive because true desires are written in the logic of their reason there can be no disagreement, only truth and error, no differences, only mistakes and lies; union is everything.

As Plato said, the word must be related to the deed.

One Thing About Retirement

I could rummage around and piss my wife off no end at the same time.

Her voice was music to my ears. "Goddamnit! Sit down. You're like an old bear. What are you looking for anyway?"

"Remember those snapshots of you when you were movie star young and beautiful? Where are they?"

"I put them in one of the upstairs closets for safekeeping. Why?"

"I was wondering if there were enough for an album."

She said, "I don't know. Happy hunting."

I didn't find the snapshots but I found an album of Polaroids of my young and movie star wife naked. They were professional, sensitive, poetic, beautiful. Only two were lascivious. I wondered when and where and who. I made a note to ask her about the album in bed that night.

Before I could ask about the album she said, "Are you awake?"

I said, "I am now."

She said, "Did you watch the evening news?"

"No."

"You should have."

"What fresh Hell did the news bring tonight?"

"This was old Hell. The News from The Past segment featured the Shirley-Corine murder-suicide. You knew them, didn't you?"

"The Pale Galilean and I were in graduate school at the same time. We were more acquaintances than friends."

My wife said, "Pale Galilean?"

I said, "That's what Shirley wanted everybody to call him."

My first real contact with The Pale Galilean was at The Dive. I was standing at the bar swilling beer when he came in and stood next to me.

After a few beers he said "I think I'll go home and bed my wife. Wanta come?"

I said, "Some other time. I've got a paper due tomorrow and a class to teach."

I'd met his wife at similar party. You could say she was about three sheets to the wind, "I'd love to be a female Praying Mantis. Imagine the thrill of biting your partner's head off after making love."

I excused myself. She left with someone not male and not her husband.

The next time I saw Shirley I was on my way to the University Book Store to steal an art book on Velazquez and Gauguin.

He said, "Got a minute?"

We ducked into the Student Union.

He said, "I'm sorry but I have to tell someone. My advisor has approved my topic for my dissertation."

"Congratulations! What might that be?"

"The effect Nietzsche's Blond Beast, Lion and Lioness, The idea of Breeding Farms, had on Nazi Germany and other governments. What do you think?"

I said, "I think I don't know anything about Nietzsche and his ideas. I plan to keep it that way."

"Why?"

"I believe people who think Nietzsche is a great thinker are fucked up."

The Pale Galilean said, "That sounds almost cruel. I had no idea you were capable of cruelty. Raye says two marks of a man are performing in bed and being capable of cruelty."

I said, "What about doing what has to be done?"

He said, "Like walking checks and cutting class and drinking beer at The Dive?"

I said, "What I had in mind was hari-kari. Excuse me."

I couldn't get rid of Shirley. He was everywhere, from sitting on the curb in front of my apartment, to leaving notes in my mail box, complaining I wouldn't talk to him, suggesting trips to Mexico at his expense. He even followed me to the Faculty Club where I was to meet a Full Professor for lunch.

Shirley excused himself, "Sir, I hope you don't mind."

The professor said, "I don't mind. What did you say your name was?"

"I didn't, but it's Shirley."

"Shirley, please have a seat. Our topic for the day is: Are homosexuals free in ways heterosexuals aren't? I think they are. What do you say, my T/A friend?"

I said, "I've only known four homosexuals very well. Only one seemed free."

One thing about Full Professors they tend to think they know everything and what's more they are not afraid to share that knowledge every chance they get. So it was with my host. He smiled, "You with the Tiresiasan name, what do you think?"

I said, "Tiresiasan?"

Shirley said, "Tiresias was a seer said to have known both sides of love. He was changed to a woman as punishment for killing two snakes while they were mating. Eight years later he ran across the same snakes doing the same thing."

I said, "Some snakes."

Shirley smiled said without missing a beat, "He killed them and became a man again.

"Juno, woman she was, mad as she was, blinded him. Since he was blind people thought he was a wise man. People came from all over to hear his truth."

I said, "Which was?"

Shirley smiled liked children will be children.

"Neither persuasion is freer than the other."

Just as I began to wonder what it would take to ruffle childlike Shirley's feathers he said, "I have some wonderful news. My wife has filed for divorce."

I said, "I don't believe it. On what grounds?"

Shirley said, "Believe it. The grounds," he said with some pride, "Physical and mental cruelty."

In some circles being accused of physical and mental cruelty was a badge of honor.

My friend the Prof said, "Mr.-Ms. Shirley, you don't look like a man capable of cruelty of any kind."

Shirley straightened, "I may not look it but I am. And proud of it. Because I am, my wife now has three lovers, me to fuck on Sunday morning, one to give her orgasms, one to pay her way to study at a sex institute in Vienna. It's wonderful."

I excused myself and left the two to their discussion.

The next time I saw Shirley was one of the few times I was in my office grading papers.

He said, "I'd like you to meet Corine, my new mattress."

Shirley smiled, "If you'll shut the door, she'll show you her breasts. They are something."

I said, "Excuse me" and shut the door.

Corine was short, dark and opulent and must have been forty-five. Shirley was right, her breasts were big and full and something.

I said, "Corine, I saw you the other day. Where was it?"

She said "I was lying on a mattress in the back of a van with a jar of Vaseline in my right hand, and a wad of dollars in my left."

Shirley said, "When things get tight Corine does her best to help out." He gave her a kiss and cupped a breast.

Corine returned the kiss and breathed deeply.

Shirley said, "Corine has left her four children and her opportunistic bastard of a husband for me. Talk about love."

Corine put her head on his chest and beamed.

Shirley said, "Wanted you two to meet. Must be going. See you later."

I thought mental cruelty must work after all.

Shirley was right about it being later. He and Corine were found dead in a rundown room in a rundown motel in Dallas.
No one knew how long they'd been there or how they got there.

Detectives speculated Shirley slit Corine's throat, then opened her up down to her pubes.

There was enough blood for Shirley to write on the wall behind their bed: Performance in bed, Capable of Cruelty, The Blond Beast, the Lion, the Lioness are proved in blood.

As far as anyone could tell Shirley emasculated himself before he slit his throat.

The media had a big time. Another day of Texas horror.

Three of us wrote the screenplay for the movie. It's still shown in Cult Film Festivals from L.A. to San Francisco to New York to Toronto to Telluride to Denver to Seattle to Dallas.

It's not a bad movie. I still haven't been paid.

Polaroids

I hadn't said a word about the Polaroids but I couldn't get them out of my mind. My wife had something else on her mind. "Our anniversary is next month."

"I know."

She said, "I know you know." Then as if it were an everyday occurrence, "Why don't we fly to Cabo, rent a cabana, eat some seafood, beachcomb, do some sightseeing, go sailing?"

The only reasons I could think of not to were money, airport security, and airline inefficiency. My wife accused me of being the most negative person she'd ever known.

So, after all the hassles over tickets, baggage and security, we learned our flight had been cancelled and our airline had failed to put us on another flight.

My first thought was so much for my Theory of Everything, but my ever smiling wife said, "No hill for a climber."

Somehow she found two seats on a flight leaving from across the terminal.

I said we'd never make it. My wife said she was going to make it come Hell or high water but that if I didn't get a move on I'd be left behind. I got a move on and we made it.

My still smiling (I'd never known her to smile so much) wife relaxed in her first class seat. Not only had she found two seats, she'd gotten us an upgrade.

We flew over some of the most beautiful mountain-desert country in the world.

I loved Mexico, had as I said even lived there for a while, but I never visited Mexico or flew over it without wondering when it was going to explode.

⟜⟝

The cabana turned out to be a small room in a small motel. One of the walls had been turned into a mural of mountains and desert. Another was covered with tapestries of Indians and cactus and eagles. The third was covered with wallpaper that had pictures of Zapata, Madero, Juarez, Pancho Villa and pretty women. The fourth wall needed painting.

We gorged on huevos con chorizo, Mexican pineapple, papaya, fruit we didn't know the name of, shrimp and crabmeat cocktails with great red sauce. We ate one plate of mariscos after another until we were on the verge of vomiting.

We played like we were beachcombers who had lost their way. I body surfed. My wife took pictures of water, water beyond water, nothing but water.

I said, "It doesn't look like we'll have time to go sailing."

My wife grinned, "Not to worry. I've rented or is it chartered a sloop for tomorrow."

The owner took one look at me and asked if I knew anything about sailing. I told him what I knew. He gave me a refresher course, had me sign all kinds of agreements and buy all kinds insurance.

In no time we were riding the swells of the Pacific.

My wife said, "It's so beautiful I feel like a new Eve in a new Garden of Eden."

"Am I a new Adam?"

"Depends on whether or not you're going go to run around naked all the time and what you think of Original Sin and the first Eve."

I said, "I've leaned my lesson about running around naked. As for Adam and Eve I've never thought their story was about sex or Original Sin. I've always thought Eve with her no-no bite of the apple opened the door to freedom and knowledge."

My wife said, "Aren't you smart?"

I pointed to the horizon, "We may find out how smart very soon. Another kind of beauty is heading our way."

The Pacific was no longer pacific. We put our life jackets on. I wondered how good they'd be if the sloop broke in two and we wound up going for a swim.

The storm was blinding and relentless. I'd never been so wet. I figured at any time the sloop would disappear and we'd be in the water. My wife's goddamned smile never looked better. I did my best to smile.

A lot of good it did. The mast broke in two.

We grabbed each other and held on. We couldn't stop shaking. I'd never known such bone rattling intensity.

I don't know how long the storm lasted or where we were when a Mexican trawler rescued us.

That night, tired and dry and no longer shaking but enjoying a candlelight dinner we joked about how our teeth chattered.

My wife said, "Did you pray?"

I said, "I thought about it. What about you?"

She said, "I didn't want to die. This may be the last sentimental thing I'll ever do. I have an album of Polaroid photographs that I want you to have, provided, you never ask me anymore about the pictures than what I'm about to tell you. Deal?"

"Deal."

"The reason I had the pictures taken is you had gone out of your way to hurt me. I thought of taking a lover and making pictures of the two of us making love. I didn't. A girl I'd met took the pictures."

I said, "She knew what she was doing. They're beautiful."

"I've wondered for the longest whether to burn the album or give it to you. I've decided to give the album to you. I hope you like them. Happy Anniversary."

I said, "Like them? I love them."

The time had come not only to tell my wife I loved her but to face not just senior moments (an expression I hated) but of going as Maugham said of Winston Churchill, Gaga.

I'd walk into a room and forget why. I'd stand and wait until it came to me. If that didn't work, I'd start over. Most of the time starting over worked.

I'd begin a story then wander off into silence.

I'd tell anyone who'd listen Geraldine was the first girl to let me hold her breasts and then have her deny she ever knew me.

I had an argument with my mirror: Does landscape is character mean the same thing as geography is personality?

I sat down at my computer and made a list of things that bothered me: retirement, me, my pot belly, gnats, mosquitoes, fire ants, termites, house payments, money, funny sounds from the disposal, dripping faucets, dry rot, ghost flushes in the front bathroom, pine needles on the roof, celebrities, lyrics to current songs, current books.

Sometimes I'd pitch a Goddamn fit. Goddamn him, goddamn her, or just goddamngoddamngoddamn.

Goddamn may not be the nicest thing to say, it may even be a sin. I doubt it. I'll wager even the Deity says Goddamn it now and then.

Goddamn like Son of a Bitch may express hopelessness, frustration, anger, disappointment, relief, happiness, pleasure, contentment, surprise, joy. More than once I've said Goddamn Son of a Bitch, goddamn, Jesus H. Christ, Mary Magdalene and all the Saints when nothing else would do.

No doubt secularism is on the increase and that's a good thing but try saying that walking down a street.

I tell this like it happened.

At my neighbor's New Year's Eve party this woman's dress was cut so low you could see the curvature of her breasts but not the nipples. Whenever she leaned forward her breasts looked like they were about to fall out. I wondered what I'd do if they did. I couldn't help but look. I could see myself trying to scoop them back in place. She said I embarrassed her.

Her husband stepped in with if you don't want men to look don't dress that way. She grabbed me and kissed me with open mouth vigor.

It was like a dream, a fantasy, a lie.

The truth is not only did it happen, she had great breasts, not too big, not too small, just right.

That's only one example.

Someone will be talking and I'll butt in, Macca, the Decider, Dwarf Planet, spring-loading, sanctimony, impossible is nothing, snowflakes, Johnny Jihad, Katrina brain vice mail, spaghetti bowl, can't get it up, four hour erection, God Wink.

When that happens, my wife looks at me like I've jumped the tracks.

She says, "I don't know. I may be wrong. You are not of this world. You are apart from it."

I say, "The hell I am. I've lived Shakespeare's "The Seven Ages of Man."

"I may have some age on me, I may be elderly, but I'm not in my second childhood. My voice does not quake. My shank may have shrunk but he is still more than a waterspout. Even if he weren't, so what?

"I may be at the cut and paste stage of life, but my imagination, though often weird, is not dead."

I asked my wife if I were to go into a coma did she think my mind would be blank or full of imagination no one could get at.

She laughed.

I have not yet jumped the tracks. I am not yet sans teeth, sans eyes, sans taste, sans everything.

There was only one thing to do, that was show the world what I was.

I painted a sign: A PART OF THE WORLD and planted it in our front yard for all to read.

Two six year old boys from the neighborhood jumped me. I grabbed them. They squealed and we rolled around on the grass, not easy for me to do.

They laughed and I felt good.

It didn't take the Association long to find out about the sign. A delegation came by and as polite as can be told me the sign had to come down. I asked why. They said It violated rule such and such.

My wife said we might as well take it down. But when An officer from the Association came by to see if we had taken it down, my wife said, "Don't you dare touch that sign. We are of this world, this life." She smiled, "People like you make me tired."

The sign didn't come down and has yet to come down.

Religious Experience

I still have trouble believing this happened, but it did.

I was getting the groceries out of the trunk of the car when this nice looking woman appeared with her mother and her child, like they had come up through the driveway.

She was big, not fat, but big, about thirty, blonde, dressed in a two piece blue suit with high heels and blue stockings. Another time I might have walked up to her, kissed her and grabbed a handful of breast.

Not now. I didn't have a chance. She said without so much as a good morning or how are you, "I'm Mrs. Adele Morgan. This is my mother Joann and this is my daughter, Jewel. We've come from the True Church of the World to talk to you about your soul." She sounded like God had already said something to her about it.

I said, "Why do you want to talk to me about my soul?"

"God wants to know if you are prepared to meet Him. What will you be like when you stand before He who rules the earth and the skies? Are you prepared for the Great Crover? Are you ready for the Afterlife? Have you a place in Heaven?"

I said, "You say God told you. Did She speak to you in English? Never mind, at this moment I am thinking more about today's appointment with my wife than I am Heaven. I wouldn't want to miss it. Today's the day. Pox Vobiscum!"

She said, "I don't want you to miss your appointment.
But I would like to give you this pamphlet, God Is Going to Get You. If you'll read it, it will help you be ready when God calls."

I remembered "The Hound of Heaven" from college. I looked to see if God were bounding down the street, looking for me.

When I turned back, the women were gone.

I wish I'd said I'm not worried about Heaven as long as there's Purgatory.

I wish I'd told Jewel there'll come a day when you won't have to go with your mother.

I was on time.

My wife was late.

My computer was giving me fits when my wife asked if she could come in. I said "Come in, I need a break."

She said, "Did you see this?" and plunked a copy of the Sunday supplement Glitter down in front of me.

I said, "No" She said "Take a good look."

Who should be on the cover but our long legged, slim, independent, vivacious, no children daughter Courtney and her over-tanned, slender, rich, inherited-wealth (he'd never done day's work in his life) husband Geek.

They had no shame. The pictures of them wrapped around each other in various ways might as well have been pictures of them making love.

That wasn't all, there was an interview with Courtney, On How to Upset Your Father:

1. When you are four beg him to run stop signs. Set up a real howl when he doesn't.
2. Convert to Christianity when you are eighteen.
3. Lie to get into China so you can save souls.
4. Laugh when he asks Why does a Christian who worships a man who said you will know the truth and the truth shall make you free believe it is necessary to lie to save souls, that "Christian" lies will save souls?
5. When a child cries at a restaurant, tell him I'll never understand why people have children.
6. Laugh when he looks at you and says I feel the same way.
7. You really want to piss him off, marry someone he doesn't want you to, especially if the husband is the beneficiary of gobs of old money and laughs at being called Geek.

Then there was Geek. The irritating thing about Geek wasn't that he was my son-in-law or that he was the oldest living idiot savant but that he loved to talk without having any idea what he was saying:

1. I believe in being user friendly.
2. I'm an adult child of dysfunctional hippie parents.
3. (Courtney got her two cents worth in. My father is the last of the dysfunctional hippie fathers.)
4. Women are not just need satisfying objects.
5. I am not into oral sadism.
6. I suffer from polymorphous perversity.
7. I am in denial and don't want to talk about it.
8. I suffer from separation anxiety.
9. I feel alienated from myself.
10. I am codependent with whatever.

The piece ended with Courtney loves Courtney, Geek loves Geek, Geek and Courtney love cats, Courtney and Geek love each other, which is as it should be.

I told my wife no wonder the world is going to Hell.

There are times my wife doesn't say anything, she just smiles and looks like she's about to head out.

When that happens my brain floods with advice from contradictory voices:

Rush in and take a chance on swamping the boat. Follow the wisdom of hold back, don't give in too quickly.

What about the pain of love rejected? Get over it?

What about the fear of love returned?

Holding back is cowardice.

Loving too much too quickly is devastating.

Love is a trick.

Don't be played a fool.

If you haven't been played a fool by now, something's wrong.

Make up your mind.

What a sadness to let love slip away.

Nothing to do but love no matter the ridicule.

For want of a nail the shoe was lost.

For want of courage love may be lost.

Smaltzy, ridiculous, but some forms of the ridiculous are worth it.

Some say The Preacher's right, "All is vanity."

So what? New things, new ideas, good and bad, are being born under the sun every day, which may not be the best reason to live but it's as good as any. So what if the world is racing downhill.

The phone rang.

Melanie, widowed, gray, no longer a spring chicken, but not dead vivacious invited me to come over, she had something she wanted to ask me. I said I love my wife. She said she'd call back when my wife wasn't there.

It's not easy to say no when barefoot Melanie cute as can be in a T-shirt that shows her nipples and shorts that leave little to your imagination invites you to come over.

I wait and wonder why she hasn't called back. Perhaps she's found another. She wouldn't have any trouble if she were looking. I'd seen her with three other men not her husband at three different times.

I don't know why but it's not easy to tell my wife I love you without sounding the fool.

I love the world, sort of.

I feel good.

I do love her.

There's nothing to do but do it. So why is it so hard?

I don't know.

I promise to tell her soon, I just don't know when.

What's a Comedy Without a Happy Ending?

A friend says no matter how it comes, silently while sleeping, quickly in a heart attack, making love in the back seat of a taxi, hit by a truck while crossing the street, in a car wreck, an airplane crash, a fire, a flood, an earthquake, falling off a horse, a cliff, one drink one snort too many, the result of a lethal injection, shot accidentally or in a rage, the true happy ending is death.

I wouldn't know about that. Death doesn't strike me as a happy ending, maybe in extreme cases like dying from an incurable, horrible disease, or just to escape.

By and large my life has been a comedy, sometimes serious, sometimes farcical, but a comedy. I suppose the time will come when I will find out if comedy is hard and dying is easy. I'm not there yet.

A good sign: My wife told me she's never thought seriously about leaving me.

A better one: I finally got around to telling my wife I love her.

I have no idea how long the harmony will last.

The sign is still in the yard.

Lagniappe

Once upon a time I believed that the failure of people to share their feelings and longings was, as a friend saidm the disappearance of female pubic hair.

I couldn't do much about the disappearance of female pubic hair. About all I could do was tell people how much I admired female pubic hair. Looking back I can see my wife was right. I was lucky I didn't wind up in a psychiatric ward, this time for God knows how long.

As it developed I didn't do much when it came to sharing feelings and longings with others.

I've about decided the only way the people will share their longings and feelings will be through a forced sameness. The same goes for my Theory of Everything.

I painted another sign: I PREFER CHAOS AND CHANCE and put it on our roof.

I wished I'd thought of the sign sooner.

Chaos and Chance

To show how chaos and chance work, I didn't know where to put these until I realized This was the place.

My wife and I were lying in bed, actually I prefer laying in bed, talking about this and that, nothing in particular, when my wife said, "Not to change the subject, Did you keep a copy of *Where the Light Is as Darkness*?"

I said, "I'm not sure. I wrote it before we married. I should have a copy but I don't have any idea where it is. I may have put it up for safekeeping, I may have given it to someone to read and they kept it. Come to think of it I gave it to you. Where is it?"

She said, "I don't know. I gave it back to you. What'd you do with it?"

I said, "I never got it back. Why the furor?"

"I'd like to read it. I've been thinking about darkness and light. I thought it might be interesting to see what you had to say. Is it a good book?"

"I wrote it, I think it is. No one else does, particularly academics and publishers. I still think it'd make a good movie."

She said, "Can you think of anyone who wrote a novel who doesn't think it'd make a good movie?"

I said, "Not in today's world."

She said, "Give me a kiss and tell me where you got the title."

I gave her a quick peck. She said, "I meant a kiss like when you were a teenager."

I said, "That's hard to do, but I'll try."

She said, "Nice try. It's a terrific title, but you still have to tell me how you came up with it."

I said, "It sounded good."

"It sounded good?"

I said, "It sounded good."

She said, "That doesn't tell me where you got the title."

I said, "Where the light is as darkness is from Job. I thought everybody knew that."

She said, "You're so smart, tell me what it means."

I said, "I could tell you it means what it means."

She said, "That would make me angry."

I said, "I don't want to do that. I'll never get over the last time I made you angry. What about night, war, love, marriage, hate, life."

She said, "All this time I thought you were trying to turn light and dark upside down. I thought you were saying darkness was hope, light was desperation. For light to equal darkness and darkness to equal light would have been something."

I said, "I didn't think you'd read the book."

She said, "You gave me a copy of the manuscript"

I said, "I did?"

She said, "You did.

I said, "I see I have some thinking to do."

She smiled, "Don't strain yourself."

I said, "I won't. Come here."

She said, "No" and hugged me.

At breakfast one Sunday, last Sunday my wife said, "I just realized I never knew who your Other Love was. You tricked me into telling you who mine was. Who was yours?"

"I never had an OL."

She said, "You never had an OL? Sexy you, God's gift to women didn't have an OL? Bullshit."

I said, "Excuse me. I have things to do."

She said, "I don't wonder."

I'd never said anything or told anyone about Rosalind. One night while Rosalind's parents were away on a sales trip, Rosalind and I lay on their couch in the living room making out with a little fondling and some heavy petting. I was lucky.

Rosalind sat up and said, "I feel like taking my clothes off."

Too shy to take her clothes off in front of me, she went to the bathroom fully clothed and came out naked.

Her smile was warm, full of trust and of the moment.

I took my clothes off and hoped her parents wouldn't show unexpectedly.

Rosalind lay back on the sofa and held her arms out to me.

The only thing she said was a soft, quiet, "That was nice. I was close. Again?"

Ever since I'd lost my virginity friends who claimed to know said if the woman didn't have an orgasm it was her lookout, what was a man supposed to do have a heart attack, it was too bad if she didn't climax, in sex it's every sex for itself, it was all right to be considerate but not too considerate, women needed to be dominated.

I forgot their wisdom and made love a second time. I needn't have worried about anyone's wisdom. Rosalind kept saying "That's it. That's it."

Her face was washed clean with pleasure, her fear and tension gone, her grip instinctive, her joy scary.

The next time I saw her she said, "Let's go rumple my parents' bed."

I may not have been all she wanted, but she went to sleep.

We dated three more times and made love each time. I was on the verge of breaking my engagement, when Rosalind said she was going to be gone for a while, I shouldn't worry, she would write. She was true to her word, I got a letter a month later.

"I hope you are well. I wanted to write you before I go.

"I like roughhouse, not so much as you, but never mind. What I liked most were the times of gentleness and tenderness. Any man can try force, you should know that, but what works most is gentleness. Being mean and cruel is not the only way to be a man. You have a lot of gentleness in you, but you're afraid of it, which is a pity.

"I know gentleness doesn't solve everything but it can work wonders. I don't mean gushy, I hate gushy. I hate pretty please with sugar on it. I hate Pollyanna.

"I love you. I'm sorry we'll never marry. I'm sorry we never decided if what we had was just sex or love.

"By the time you get this letter I'll be gone forever, excuse the romantic bullshit."

She was right, by the time I got her letter she was gone, as she said, forever.

Sometimes I cry when I think of her.

You ever wonder about the force of a lie and what it does?

I do.

My first serious lie got me admitted to graduate school and an appointment as a T/A.

My second serious lie brought me Rosalind for a while.

My third serious lie? A happy marriage.

There was time when I was writing for Suppressed Desires I believed in the efficacy of lying.

I went so far as to write, "You have heard it said you shall know the truth and the truth shall make you free, but I am here to tell you, you shall know the lie and the lie shall make you free."

All it took for me to change my mind was to learn I was not a good liar. I suppose you could say I believe that somehow the truth, whatever it is, will make me free.

Yet, in some ways I'm proud of my blasphemous thoughts.

Here's to Chaos and Chance, to desert flowers, the law of Unintended Consequences and Keeping On.

Not to forget, what is it, Love.

Epilogue

I ran across this when I was looking for something else. I suppose there are those who would call it serendipity. I'm not sure I would.

Here it is just as I found it.

Why am I not dead? Perhaps I soon will be. I wouldn't be surprised if it happened in the next six months.

Intrusion. It didn't.

A general wseariness (sic), an inability to walk, a subtle increase in my fasting blood sugar readings, a fatigue bringing body, m9nd (sic) and spirits wdown (sic). A muscatel homeliness, an overall failure of heart and will, an engulfing self pity, the disappearance of energy, optimism, a desire to work, to produce, an over abiding that nothing is worth the effort, a feeling of more than what the fuck, a feeling truly of what the fuck, let the lion and the bear fight over and devour the body, See, all is lost when such bullshit pours out so easily

Shame shame shame shame

Bye bye bye.

Ffff f

a dead moment not to be awaken, not to be aware of any eternity or thing, but a ceasing, an unrecognized dissipated energfy (sic), even though that isn't what I meant. Stp Stoppage, thet (sic) and that and nothing more.

I'm not sure what I meant when I wrote it, but I thought I'd put it here just in case I ever remembered what I meant.

CPSIA information can be obtained at www.ICGtesting.com
Printed in the USA
LVOW131554060912

297647LV00001B/196/P

[7]